Awesome Blossom
A Flower Power Book

Lauren Myracle

Amulet Books · New York

Library of Congress Cataloging-in-Publication Data

Myracle, Lauren, 1969–
Awesome Blossom : a Flower power book / by Lauren Myracle.
p. cm.
Summary: Fifth-grade best friends Katie-Rose, Milla, Yasaman, and Violet are determined to save a new student from Modessa's evil influence, but Katie-Rose is busy not flirting with Preston and all four are distracted by trying to organize Yasaman's sister's birthday party.
ISBN 978-1-4197-0405-5
[1. Best friends—Fiction. 2. Friendship—Fiction. 3. Birthday parties—Fiction. 4. Schools—Fiction. 5. California—Fiction.] I.
Title.
PZ7.M9955Awe 2013
[Fic]—dc23
2012035668

The text in this book is set in 11-point The Serif Light. The display typefaces are Annabelle, Chalet, FMRustlingBranches, RetrofitLight, Shag, and TriplexSans.

Text copyright © 2013 Lauren Myracle
Illustrations copyright © 2009–13 Christine Norrie
Book design by Maria T. Middleton

Printed and bound in U.S.A.
10 9 8 7 6 5 4 3 2 1

ABRAMS
THE ART OF BOOKS SINCE 1949

115 West 18th Street
New York, NY 10011
www.abramsbooks.com

For

Campbell,
Hannah, Hayley,
and Oona.

Y'all are so special to me!

Sunday, November 13

The Flower Box

Yasaman:	hi!!!! +waves at friends+
Yasaman:	+puts hand down+
Yasaman:	+looks all around for friends+
Yasaman:	um . . . friends? are you there?
Yasaman:	Milla?
Yasaman:	Violet?
Yasaman:	Katie-Rose????
Yasaman:	really?!!! No one's online? NO ONE? A travesty, I say!
Yasaman:	well, I *suppose* I'll forgive you, since you

were all so super a lot AWESOME today, helping out with Nigar's bubble-gum party. omigoodness, Nigar—my very own little sister—is 4 now! +puts hand on chest+ how fast they grow up. cluck, cluck, cluck.

Yasaman: wait, that sounds wrong. not cluck cluck cluck. That makes me sound like a chicken!

Yasaman: I *meant* to say tsk tsk! Oh, how fast they grow up, those littlies! Tsk tsk tsk!

Yasaman: anyway, her party really was awesome, and Nigar is on cloud nine and thinks y'all are like the coolest people ever. Also, she is right. Also, she is hopped up on sugar from the bubble-gum scavenger hunt. 200 bubble-gum balls!!! We hid 200 bubble-gum balls!!!! I am so impressed with us!

Yasaman: Nigar loved the scavenger hunt, AND she loved pin-the-wrapper-on-the-stick-of-gum, but her favorite part of the party was all the bubble-gum names. She wants us to turn them into our REAL names!

Yasaman: so whaddaya say, Katie-Yum? Millaburst, I know you're in, right? Hee hee.

Yasaman: as for you, Violets. +makes stern face+ I mean, I get it—Chiclets, Violets—but I think Katie-Rose, I mean Katie-YUM, was right on that one being kinda lame.

Yasaman: but Nigar insisted we call her Princess Bubblelina for the whole day. I heard my dad say that "silly is fine for a day, but not forever." I'm guessing Princess Bubblelina will wake up tomorrow and be normal old Nigar again . . . 😐

Yasaman: as for us, back to normal old normal tomorrow, too? after pulling off another excellent FFF mission—Project Nigar's B-Day Party, checked off and done! yay, us!!!!—some plain old normalness sounds pretty good!

Yasaman: see you in the morning, my bestest bubbly buddies ever!!!!

Monday, November 14

One

Camilla

Yasaman, Violet, Katie-Rose, and Camilla are indeed the bestest of bubbly buddies ever. They're BBBs! That makes Milla smile: BBBs instead of FFFs, which is the abbreviation the girls usually use to describe themselves, which stands for Flower Friends Forever. Why flower friends? Because of their names. Katie-Rose and Violet, those need no explaining. Yasaman is trickier, but not much: "Yasaman" means "jasmine" in Turkish. As for Milla? Well, a camilla is a sweet pink flower that grows along the edges of streams. And there you have it! Four best friends, all with flower names. Take "BFFs," switch out the "B," put in an "F," and what do you get?

Bingo! Or . . . fingo? No, that's something Katie-Rose would say. Katie-Rose is the spazziest of the FFFs, and while Katie-Rose's spazzy energy GETS THINGS DONE, Milla is more of a quiet sort of girl. Not *shy*, exactly. Yaz is the shyest of the flowers, though not as much now as she used to be. Milla is okay with peacefulness and smooth sailing and untroubled waters. Milla likes the idea of being an unassuming flower growing sweetly by the edge of a sweetly burbling stream, and so, like Yaz, she is totally up for some plain old normalness after yesterday's tornado of swirling, twirling, bubble-gum-popping four-year-olds.

The morning goes without a hitch. Milla sees Max, her semisecret semi-boyfriend (*boyfriend!* Eeek!) and smiles at him. He grins back. She flutters her fingers at him. He waves back. It is all very happy-making.

Then comes lunch, and at first, everything does seem normal. Milla sits with Yaz, Katie-Rose, and Violet, and together they create a delicious bouquet of chatter and interruptions, silliness and shoulder thwacks. All that plus an abundance of apple slices, organic Greek yogurt, and yummy-in-the-tummy gummi bears, which Katie-Rose has a whole bag of, and which she shares liberally.

Katie-Rose packs her own lunch. That's why she often shows up with stuffed-to-the-brim plastic bags of candy. Occasionally she throws in a PB&J or a handful of cheese sticks for good measure, but she's just as likely to fill her entire Betty Boop lunch box with snack bags of Fritos and SunChips. It is incredible, really, how much food Katie-Rose packs in, especially given how tiny she is.

Only sometimes, when Katie-Rose eats too many gummi bears (or green apple sour loops or grape Pixy Stix or Oatmeal Creme Pies), she gets even more hyper than usual. Like now. She's telling a story about her brothers' obsession with farting (gross!), and she's talking crazy fast, at least a thousand words a minute as opposed to her usual hundred words a minute, and a droplet of *spit*, real live spit, flies out of her mouth and lands—*sploop!*—on Yasaman's tabouleh.

"Ew," Yaz says, nudging the tabouleh away.

"And then, if you don't say 'safety,' you have to go touch the toilet or get punched, whichever the other person says," Katie-Rose goes on.

Violet looks at Milla. "What is she blathering about?"

"Some new middle school game?" Milla says. "Where if you, um, make a smelly, you have to say 'safety' or"— she wrinkles her nose—"go touch the toilet?"

"Make a *smelly*?" Violet says. She laughs.

Milla blushes. She, for one, is glad to be safely in the fifth grade, where such games don't exist. Or smellies. Or at least not too many smellies, except for when certain boys are around. Boys like Chance and Preston, who throw erasers and wear skater-dude duds and tilt their chairs onto the back two legs and sometimes fall over. And laugh hysterically.

Max does none of those things, thank goodness.

"She spit in my tabouleh," Yaz says. She looks from Violet to Milla.

"—and *then*, if you do say 'safety,' but the other person doesn't hear, you have to touch the toilet *and* go tell the girl you have a crush on what you just did!" Katie-Rose says, wide-eyed. "Can you believe that?"

"No," Violet says. "There are too many loopholes in that game. I would just lie and say I didn't say it. Or lie and say I did. One or the other."

Katie-Rose reaches for another handful of gummi bears and gets them within inches of her wide-open mouth before Violet slaps her hand. "Hey!"

"Drop the gummi bears, and no one will get hurt," Violet commands.

"But—"

"You heard her," Milla says.

"You spit on my tablouleh," Yaz says.

"I did not!" Katie-Rose protests.

Yaz points to the offending droplet. It is a miniature crystal of saliva, teardrop shaped. It would be pretty if it weren't made out of spit.

Katie-Rose's face falls, and she lets the gummi bears fall, too. "Safety?" she says in a small voice.

"I'm not going to make you touch the toilet!" Yaz says. She adjusts her headscarf. "Yuck! Just . . . no more spitting, 'kay?"

Katie-Rose heaves a sigh. "*Fine*, but sometimes you all are so *boring*."

"Did you want Yaz to make you touch the toilet?" Violet asks.

Milla, who would prefer not to be discussing toilets and spit, glances around Rivendell Elementary's commons. The commons is a large, open space scattered with tables, fold-out metal chairs, and battered sofas. It's where the two fifth-grade classrooms come together for assemblies, and it's where, on Monday afternoons, all the grades gather for group sing. It's also where Rivendell kids eat when it's too chilly to go outside.

She spots Natalia Totenburg prying a bit of food out of her ginormous and elaborately wired headgear. She spots Preston sprinkling pepper into Chance's milk. She spots Modessa, Rivendell's power-hungry queen bee, as well as Modessa's followers, a snarky beanpole of a girl named Quin and a girl in pink cowboy boots named Elena.

Elena used to be nice, but now she's not. Now she's one of the three Evil Chicks, which is what Modessa, Quin, and Elena call themselves. In one of far too many episodes of the Modessa Wars, the flower friends tried to keep Elena from joining Modessa's evil forces. They reasoned with her. They said, "Don't be a dummy-head! Modessa and Quin are mean!" They reminded her again and again that she was a NICE GIRL, and Milla even used secret eye signals to say, "Do you need rescuing? Because here I am! Ready to rescue you!"

But nothing worked. They didn't rescue her. They failed. The hardest part to swallow is that Milla knows in her heart that Elena isn't happy, can't possibly be happy, and yet . . . there she is, still with Modessa and Quin.

The FFFs failed to save her, and it continues to fill Milla with regret.

Well, there's nothing she can do about it now, so she moves her gaze to the next table. Immediately, her sadness turns into surprise. "Who . . . ," she tries to say. "Who . . . who . . . ?"

"Are you an owl?" Katie-Rose asks.

Milla points a finger at a nearby table. "Who's that?!"

Yaz, Katie-Rose, and Violet turn their heads, and their expressions tell Milla that they see her, too: a new girl, with curly red hair, pale skin, and a crop of freckles scattered across her nose and cheeks. She has pierced ears, which isn't exactly a novelty among Rivendell's fifth graders (Violet has pierced ears), but which certainly isn't the norm. She's sitting by herself, a single star in the midst of a galaxy of constellations.

"Oh yeah," Violet says. "I meant to tell y'all."

"Tell us what?" Katie-Rose says.

"Her name's Hayley," Violet says. She looks at Milla. "She's going to be in Mr. Emerson's class with us."

"She is?" Milla says.

"How do you know her and we don't?" Yaz says.

"I *don't* know her," Violet says.

"Then how do you know her name?" Katie-Rose says, regarding Violet and pooching out her lips in a disapproving way. "How do you know she exists?"

"She exists because there she is," Violet says. "And I was at the office when she first got here. She just moved to Thousand Oaks. She's from … somewhere."

"Wow, so helpful," Katie-Rose says.

"What is she like?" Milla asks. "Did you talk to her?"

Violet gets a strange look on her face. "Uh-oh," she says. "Trouble." She gestures with her chin, directing the flower friends' attention back to Hayley. "Look."

Katie-Rose, Yasaman, and Milla re-swivel their heads. Milla's eyes widen.

"That is so wrong," Milla murmurs, because one minute ago, Hayley sat alone. Now Modessa and Quin are sitting on either side of her. They're *talking* to her, and she's talking back. And now Elena, the third Evil Chick, is pulling out the remaining chair at Hayley's table. She plops down and props her elbows on the table.

"No," Milla says. "No, no, no."

"Looks more like *yes*," Katie-Rose says. "Yes, yes, yes."

"Poor girl!" Yaz says. "She should *not* have let them sit with her! She doesn't know them yet, or how mean they are."

Modessa smirks and jabs her finger in the direction of Hayley's chest, saying something Milla can't make out.

"She's about to find out," Milla murmurs.

"Hmm," Violet says in a tight sort of way. "Is she?"

Milla doesn't understand, so she studies Hayley and the Evil Chicks more closely. She sees that Modessa is no longer smirking. She's grinning. Quin seems confused, as if she's teetering between smirking and grinning. Elena does neither. She leans forward and listens intently to whatever Hayley is saying.

And how weird. It's Hayley—not Modessa, not Quin, and not Elena—who's doing all the talking now. What happens next is even weirder, because Hayley adopts a take-no-prisoners expression and jabs *her* finger at *Modessa*.

The flower friends suck in their breath as one.

There is a heavy moment in which anything could happen. Modessa could draw back and narrow her eyes. She could make some mean, horrible remark—she keeps mean, horrible remarks in her pocket like other kids keep coins or rumpled tissues—and make Hayley burst into tears. She could even storm off in a big and dramatic way, leaving Hayley humiliated and alone.

But instead, *Modessa busts out laughing*. Real laughter, by the look of it, as opposed to the cruel, witchy, Evil Chick laughter Milla would have expected. Next, Elena laughs, and finally Quin. Hayley laughs along with them, just for a moment. Then her laughter trickles off and she smiles a mysterious, closed-lipped smile.

Weird. Very, very weird. It sets Milla on edge, because

"Modessa" and "non-cruel laughter" are not terms that normally go together.

Milla catches her lower lip between her teeth. It appears that the gift of "plain old normalness" isn't in the cards for the flower friends, not even for a day.

Two

Mr. Emerson, Violet's fifth-grade teacher, is explaining a writing assignment. Violet wants to hear what he's saying, because she loves writing, so she glares at Thomas, who thinks it's far more important to play with his annoying "sonic screwdriver" (whatever the heck a sonic screwdriver is!) than to pay attention to Mr. E.

As far as fifth-grade boys go, Thomas is basically a good guy . . . not that that's saying much. The best thing about Thomas, in Violet's opinion, is that he is Max's friend, and Max is Milla's semisecret semi-boyfriend. Therefore, by virtue of association, Violet likes Thomas well enough, she supposes. She still wishes he would shut it.

"Dude," Thomas whispers to Max. "Check it." With his thumb, he pushes a switch on his sonic screwdriver. The end of the screwdriver expands and unfolds, making four small blades spring open like petals. When Thomas nudges the switch again, the blades twirl rapidly, emitting a low hum.

"You love it, don't you, dude?" Thomas says to Max.

Max sighs. He is the sort of fifth grader who likes to pay attention to his teacher, too. "Yes, Thomas. I love it. I love it so much, I want to marry it."

Thomas chortles. "*Dude!* That is *so* wrong!"

Max sighs again. Violet sighs, too. The truth is, she'd be struggling to pay attention to Mr. E even without the distraction of Thomas and his sonic screwdriver. Why? Because she can't get that new girl—Hayley—out of her mind, especially since *Hayley is now in Mr. Emerson's very classroom with her.*

Right after lunch, while Mr. Emerson was drilling everyone on math facts, Rivendell's principal escorted Hayley to Mr. Emerson's room. Gone was Hayley's cryptic smile from lunch. Her hands were jammed into the back pockets of her jeans, and her shoulders were hunched.

She's nervous, Violet thought. *Then again, a roomful of strangers is staring at her. Anyone would be nervous.*

"Ms. Dub," Mr. Emerson had called out to their principal, because that's what he calls Ms. Westerfeld. Because of the "W." Sometimes he calls her *Ms. Rub-a-Dub-Dub, Three Principals in a Tub*, but only to his students. "What can I do for you?"

"Mr. Emerson, students, this is Hayley Green," Ms. Westerfeld said in her smooth principal's voice. "Hayley is new to Rivendell. Today is her first day, and I know you'll make her feel welcome."

"Fantastic," Mr. E said. "Glad to have you, Hayley."

"Hayley, why don't you go on and find a seat?" Ms. Westerfeld said, gesturing vaguely in Violet's direction. Violet's stomach tightened, but she wasn't sure why. There was an empty desk between Violet and Cyril Remkiwicz, but why should Violet care if Hayley sat there? At any rate, it wasn't as if Violet had any say in the matter.

"John, can I speak with you for a moment?" Ms. Westerfeld asked Mr. Emerson.

"You bet," Mr. Emerson said, hopping off his desk and crossing the room. He and Ms. Westerfeld stepped into the hall. Their voices were low. Murmuring.

The new girl—Hayley—pressed her lips together. She met no one's eyes as she strode across the room, and sure enough, she chose the empty desk by Violet. She's been sitting there, still as a rock, ever since Mr. E returned from his whispered conference with the principal.

Math facts ended. Journal writing began. It's been an hour since Hayley was ushered into the classroom, and she hasn't looked at Violet yet. Nor, for that matter, has Violet looked at her.

Violet hasn't been able to stop thinking about her, though. Thinking about her and feeling . . . well . . . worried about her. She wishes she weren't, but Violet is one smart cookie, and she has learned some things over the course of her ten years. (Plus, she's gone to therapy. It had to do with her mom, but her mom is better now. Mainly.)

Violet can sum up her life philosophy in three major points:

• When you hide stuff from yourself, like when you

can't help thinking about something (like Hayley) and you tell yourself you AREN'T thinking about that thing, even when you are, it just makes things worse.

- Emotions are not decisions. You don't have to act on them. You just have to feel them.
- AND you can get better and better at dealing with your emotions when they come up, and doing so can help you be a better person.

Heavy stuff for a fifth grader, Violet knows. But so it goes, right? It's not as if you get to choose your life. The best you can do is choose how to live it.

All of which goes back to Violet's policy of trying to be honest with her own thoughts and emotions, at least when it comes to admitting them to herself. And yes: Violet is worried about Hayley. Worried that Hayley will fall into the wrong crowd at Rivendell before she even has a chance to learn who the right crowd consists of.

". . . so what's this week's writing assignment?" Mr. Emerson asks, pulling Violet back to the moment.

"To write a poem!" Becca calls out.

"Yes!" Mr. Emerson says, pointing at Becca as if she's won a prize. He only uses his right hand to point at people, because he doesn't have a left hand. For that matter, he doesn't have a left arm, so how *could* he have a left hand? "Excellent, Becca. And the theme of the poem?"

"The Bay of Pigs!" Thomas shouts.

Mr. Emerson points at Thomas as if *he's* won a prize. His tone is equally cheery, though his words are the opposite. "No! Wrong!"

"Doctor Who!" Thomas shouts. *Doctor Who* is a British television show that Thomas is currently obsessed with, and it's the real Doctor Who who owns a sonic screwdriver. The real Doctor Who's sonic screwdriver can open just about any lock, act as a medical scanning device, distract giant maggots, make an alien's mask fall off, and destroy a Dalek's brain. And that's just a small, *small* sampling of what it can do, which Violet has the misfortune of knowing because Thomas is very persistent in his attempts to educate the whole fifth grade about his hero and his hero's gadgets.

"No!" Mr. Emerson cries. "*Ding ding ding*, give the boy a sock monkey, because *no*, young sir, the theme of the poem is *not* Doctor Who!" He scans the room. "Someone else want to take a go at it?"

"Do I really get a sock monkey?" Thomas asks.

"You do not." Mr. Emerson zeroes in on his star pupil. "Violet. The theme of the poetry assignment, please?"

Violet blinks. "Um . . . who we are, and how we got to be that way?"

"Yes, my darling girl, that is correct," Mr. Emerson says. "Although to clarify, you will not be writing about your*selves*, plural, as in the youth of America, or the fifth graders of Rivendell, or even the fifth graders in the dashing and brilliant Mr. Emerson's class. Instead, you'll be exploring, in words, your own perfect and unique identity. And yes, that even applies to you, Thomas."

Everyone laughs.

"And the title of your poem should be . . .?"

Milla raises her hand. "'Where I'm From'?"

"'Where I'm From,'" Mr. Emerson repeats. "That's right, Meal Worm. Very good."

"Meal Worm" is a newish nickname Mr. Emerson has given Milla, and Milla blushes as other kids echo Mr. Emerson's sentiments:

"*Ding ding ding!* A sock monkey for Meal Worm!" says Thomas.

"Yeah, a sock monkey for Meal Worm!" Carmen Glover repeats.

Violet gives Carmen a *look*. Not for being unoriginal but for teasing sweet Milla. Anyway, Carmen Glover is a known and card-carrying nose picker, and that's just gross.

"Right, then, let's get started," Mr. Emerson says. Other teachers clap their hands to get their students' attention, but Mr. E lifts a whistle that dangles from a cord around his neck and gives it a sharp blast. "Take out your journals, please, and begin brainstorming. And remember, brainstorming isn't a right or wrong activity"—he eyeballs Thomas—"*unless* you focus exclusively on Doctor Who."

Thomas thrusts his fists into the air. "I am a Time Lord! I am an extraterrestrial from the planet Gallifrey. That's where *I'm* from!"

"Just let whatever comes out, come out," Mr. Emerson says. "Except you, Thomas. Now get to work, if you would be so kind."

Violet stares at her paper. She doodles a tulip in the

margin. Tulips are easy to draw: just a "U" and three points at the top. Adding a stem and petals is easy-peasy. *Where am I from?* she thinks. Well, Atlanta, of course. She moved here, to Thousand Oaks, California, at the beginning of the school year. But what city you're from . . . is that what Mr. Emerson means?

She glances at the new girl's paper. Nothing. Not even any doodles. Not even her name at the top right corner.

Violet hesitates, then blows out the breath she didn't realize she was holding. She puts down her pencil and leans toward Hayley's desk. After all, Violet was the new girl once, and not that long ago.

"Hi," she whispers. "I'm Violet."

"I'm Hayley," the new girl says. She cuts her eyes at Mr. Emerson, who's taking care of busywork at his desk. "What's with him?"

"With Mr. Emerson?" Violet says. "What do you mean?

"Is his name Mr. Emerson?" Hayley shrugs, as if it's not the name she would have given him. "What happened to his arm?"

Violet grows defensive, forgetting that she was startled by Mr. Emerson's folded-over-and-sewn-up sleeve the first time she saw it, too. "He was in a car accident."

Once more, Hayley seems less than satisfied with Violet's answer, as if she was hoping for something better, maybe a shark attack or a run-in with a piece of grinding machinery.

She jerks her chin past Mr. Emerson's desk. "What about that oar thing? What's up with that?"

"It's a kayak oar," Violet explains. "It's the bathroom pass."

"It's ... big. *Really* big."

Violet starts to defend Mr. E's bathroom pass—it's funny! What other teacher uses a kayak oar for a bathroom pass?—then changes her mind. She mimics Hayley's own slightly bored expression and cocks her head. *It's big, all right,* she says silently, but with enough attitude that Hayley can probably get the gist. *Good powers of observation.*

Hayley looks away first. "Disturbing," she mutters.

Violet would have to agree, *if* they were referring to the same thing. But they're not. Hayley's talking about the bathroom pass, while Violet is thinking about Hayley.

Three

There is a sandstorm swirling inside Yasaman, hot and dry and needle sharp.

She's mad that Modessa and her Evil Chick followers
are trying to cozy up to the new girl. Though "cozy" is the
last word she would use to describe Modessa or Quin or—
it's sad to say—Elena.

There was a time when Yaz *would* have said that Elena
was cozy, or had cozy potential. Elena used to be just a
nice, normal girl. She and her parents live on a small farm,
and Elena used to tell Yaz about the llamas they raised.
How cute they were, and how one llama in particular

would make a funny wuffling sound when Elena fed him. His name was Henry, Yaz remembers, and he always tried to eat Elena's shirt.

Yaz never met Henry—she's never been to Elena's farm—but an image of Henry pops into Yasaman's mind nonetheless. Henry the Imaginary Llama has huge dark eyes with lashes that curl up at the ends. Henry the Imaginary Llama has soft brown skin ... or fur ...? Yes, fur. Soft brown fur with a few white spots and a wet nose and adorable ears with foldy-over tips.

Henry the Imaginary Llama blinks at Yasaman in her daydream and communicates with her telepathically: *I miss the real Elena. She never lets me nibble her shirt anymore. What happened to her? What happened to my friend?*

Yaz shakes her head. *I don't know,* she responds silently. *Just that Modessa got to her, that's all. She weaseled her way into Elena's brain. First at recess—far too many places to get a girl alone. Then during lunch one day, and then the next and the next—except "skipping" days every so often with no rhyme or reason, just to mess with Elena's mind. Flattery sometimes. Other times, cruelty, like Modessa saying how lucky it was that Elena goes to a private school where bullying isn't allowed, or she'd be spending most of her time shoved in a locker. "Ha ha, kidding. I'd beat up anyone who tried that, dummy."*

Yaz's muscles tighten. She'll never know the full ins and outs of Elena's transformation. All that matters is that Modessa got to her—*bullied* her, despite Rivendell's anti-bully policy!—and changed her.

What if the new girl has coziness potential, and Modessa snuffs it out just like she snuffed it out in Elena? What if the new girl has a pet—not a llama, probably, but maybe a kitten or a goldfish—and the new girl stops giving it attention, and it falls into a kitten-goldfish depression and stops eating, and its fur-slash-scales fall out in clumps?

Thinking about it makes Yasaman grip the book she's supposed to be reading more tightly than she needs to. It makes Yaz want to fling her book onto the floor, even, and Yaz is *not* a book-flinging sort of girl.

The new girl and her soon-to-be-depressed kitten-goldfish aren't the only things making Yasaman mad, however. She's also mad at Natalia Totenburg, a perfectly nice girl who's in Ms. Perez's class with her. Why? Because it's silent reading time, and Natalia is not being silent. Natalia has a head cold, and she keeps sniffling. Every five seconds, she sniffs, and there's a dampness to the sniffs that makes Yaz's toes curl. If Natalia needs a Kleenex, Yaz thinks, then she should slide out of her desk and go get one. There's a box on Ms. Perez's desk, just like always. The tissue sticking out of the box is white and soft looking, its corner flopping over in a totally nonthreatening way. It reminds Yaz of something . . . but what? *Oh!* It reminds her of Henry the Imaginary Llama's sweet foldy-over ear, that's what.

Yaz shakes her head, grumpy at all the weird thoughts running through her head. She's mad at them, too, and she wants them to *leave*. But they don't, that's the thing. The weird thoughts *are* the sandstorm whirling beneath her skin. The weird thoughts *and* the grumpy thoughts *and* the mad thoughts—they've clustered together and are poking her from the inside.

What makes it worse is that Yaz is not, by nature, an angry person. That means she doesn't know how to handle these foreign emotions. Nobody's ever taught her. Nobody's ever *needed* to teach her.

Yesterday, I was the bubble-gum queen, she thinks, *and today I'm a stupid sandstorm. What is* wrong *with me? Is it growing pains? Are my bones growing too fast and making my nerves and cells and muscles go haywire?*

She drums her fingers against her desk without realizing it. She hears the annoying *barump barump barump* of fingertips against wood, but it's not until she scowls and searches for the source of that ANNOYING NOISE that she realizes it's coming from her. *She's* making the annoying noise, and it's even more annoying than Natalia's constant sniffing.

Whoa. Yaz has to get a grip on herself, because Yasaman is Yasaman, and Yasaman does not make annoying noises.

She straightens her spine and tries to focus on her book. That's what the unsandy Yaz would do. The unsandy Yaz likes to read, and the unsandy Yaz likes to please her teacher, Ms. Perez, who is one of her favorite people in the world. The unsandy Yaz would never want to disappoint Ms. Perez by not being perfect, never ever ever.

Ms. Perez lifts her head and smiles at Yaz, almost as if she knows what Yaz is thinking. *Does she? Could she?*

No. People can't read other people's minds, not unless they're on TV shows.

Yaz smiles shakily back at her teacher. Ms. Perez is wearing a snazzy black top today, and she looks super cute. Some kids—*cough cough* Modessa and Quin *cough cough*—say Ms. Perez is fat, but she's not. She's huggable. She has curves. And she has shiny butterscotch highlights in her dark hair, which bring out the glow of her brown skin. She's beautiful, that's what she is, and Yaz suspects that the other fifth-grade teacher, Mr. Emerson, is secretly in love with her. If he's not, he should be.

Yaz is having no luck focusing on her novel, so she gets out her vocabulary book and decides to get a head start on the next lesson. Books, you have to focus fully on. Vocabulary? Not so much.

She opens her workbook:

1. Come up with a word that rhymes with "trod" and use it in a sentence.

Easy enough. My flower power pod has never trod on anyone. (Well, mainly. *Maybe* Modessa. *Maybe* a little.)

2. Using the dictionary in the back of your work-

book, look up the definition of the word "enigmatic." Use "enigmatic" in an original sentence.

Okeydoke. "Enigmatic. Adjective. Perplexing or mysterious." A *person could be enigmatic, and maybe other people won't know what to make of that person; nonetheless, you shouldn't jump to conclusions, because that person could be nice or mean, and you just won't know until you see how she acts later.* Yaz is proud of her use of the semicolon, which she had to use in order to keep her sentence a single sentence. She hopes Ms. Perez appreciates it.

Yaz puffs her chest with air, then blows it all out. She's feeling less sandy. She's feeling better, and feeling better makes her feel … *better.* She giggles, and Ms. Perez regards her inquisitively.

"Yaz?" she asks. "Everything all right?"

"Absolutely. Um, yes." She blushes. "Sorry for laughing."

"No worries. But since you've put away your free reading book, will you run an errand for me, honey?"

"I will!" Preston calls.

"*I* will!" Chance yells. "I can put away my free reading

book, too!" He holds it up, waggles it, and thrusts it in his desk. "See? Here I am, putting it away!"

Yaz pays no attention to them, and neither does Ms. Perez. They know that Preston and Chance just want to get out of class.

Yaz slips out of her desk and goes to her teacher. "What do you need me to do?" she asks.

Ms. Perez scribbles some sentences onto a piece of notebook paper, folds the paper four times, and holds it out to Yasaman. "Would you deliver this to Mr. Emerson, please?"

Yaz accepts the note. She trips over Modessa's feet on her way to the door, and Modessa says, "Oops, sorry."

Yaz doesn't respond.

Quin snickers, and so does Elena. Yaz ignores Quin, just as she ignored Modessa. But she shocks herself by looking straight at Elena.

Don't you remember Henry the Llama? Yaz says to Elena silently. *Don't you want to be nice again instead of mean?*

Elena's snickers die off. Her expression wobbles.

Yaz bows her head, because it's too raw and too wrong.

Her gaze lands on Elena's spiral notebook, which is filled with a back-and-forth conversation.

so? new girl?

That's Modessa's handwriting. After years of going to school with Modessa, Yaz knows her handwriting.

I dunno. She seems cool, I guess. Or not. Um, what do you think?

That's Elena. Even if Yaz didn't recognize Elena's handwriting, the "what do you think?" would give it away. Because Modessa doesn't ask. Modessa tells.

I think it's interesting how interested other people are in her. Did you see Violet staring during lunch? Violet and her posse of mud worms?

Mud worms? Yaz thinks. The Evil Chicks call Yaz and her flower friends "mud worms"???

She keeps reading, skimming as much as she can as fast as she can. Luckily, Chance and Preston have started a loudly whispered round of "the game," which involves trading remarks like, "You just lost the game!" "No, *you* did, turd-breath!" Everyone, including Ms. Perez and also Elena, turn to look. It buys Yaz some time.

But listen, E. We are NOT going to let the mud worms have Hayley. NO. WAY.

Have her? What do you mean?

Really, E? Really?!!

~~I just meant~~ Do you want her to be an Evil Chick, then?

Yet to be determined. Her hair's a nightmare, but she could always wear a hat. Or a paper bag.

"Nosy much?" Modessa says, making Yaz jump. But at least it unfreezes her legs. Clutching the folded-over note Ms. Perez asked her to deliver to Mr. Emerson, Yaz hurries out of the room. Her heart is a trapped animal, heavy and thumping. Drumming out a message: *no, no, no.*

Yasaman doesn't know Hayley any better than Modessa does. In fact, she knows her less well, having yet to exchange a single word with her. But it doesn't matter. Yaz *does* know Modessa, and Modessa *will* invite Hayley to be Evil Chick number four.

It will be up to the flower friends to make sure Hayley says no.

four

K atie-Rose loves Yaz. Katie-Rose does not love
Medusa, a.k.a. the evil Modessa. So when Yaz
phones Katie-Rose to have an after-school chat, at first
Katie-Rose is like, "Yay! Yasaman! Love my bestie!" But
when she realizes that all Yaz wants to talk about is
Modessa and Modessa's latest plan to ruin the world,
she's like, "Boo. *Boo!!!*"

Why? Because they have been down this road before,
Katie-Rose and Yaz.

The first Modessa battle played out at the beginning
of the school year, and it had to do with Modessa and

Camilla. Milla—once upon a *very* long time ago—was part of Modessa's clique. Helping Milla escape from Modessa's clutches was sort of a big part of how Yaz and Katie-Rose became friends, so maybe that particular Modessa battle needed to happen and was even fated to happen. Maybe.

The next Modessa battle had to do with Violet, who stood up to Modessa when she was picking on weird Cyril Remkiwicz. The FFFs won that battle just as squarely and awesomely as they won the first battle, so *ha*.

But then, last month, another Modessa battle reared its ugly head. Seriously! This time it was about Elena, and how Modessa was trying to steal Elena's soul and turn her into a Modessa clone. Which she succeeded in doing. Which sucks. But Elena *does* (or did) have a brain. Elena could have put her foot down (on top of Modessa's! Ha! That would have been epic!). And she could have kept wearing jeans and button-downs, which looked like cowgirl clothes to Katie-Rose, and which Katie-Rose always secretly admired, because she wouldn't mind being a cowgirl herself, only without the cows.

Elena could have stayed herself, but no. The "new"

Elena wears skirts and cute little tops now, and beneath her tops are the obvious bumps of bra straps. Stupid, stupid, stupid. Elena still wears her cowboy boots on occasion, but paired with her new style, they look . . . well . . . stylish. Again, stupid, stupid, stupid.

Does Katie-Rose wish Modessa *hadn't* blown her poisonous un-fairy dust all over Elena? Sure. Of course. But there's nothing Katie-Rose or Yaz can do about it *now*. They can't go back in time and vacuum it up, obviously.

Elena made her bed and now she has to lie in it, as Katie-Rose's mom would say. And the flower friends should let her—that's what Katie-Rose would say. And she has! Repeatedly. Katie-Rose has also repeatedly shared her opinion that it would be far more FUN to just, you know, focus on being flower friends forever and forget about any and all annoying classmates.

But Yaz refuses to listen, because Yaz has a *huuuuge* heart. So now, in addition to being concerned about Elena, she's all concerned about this new girl, this Hayley person, and . . . *blah*. It's just so annoying.

"—fake laugh, maybe. Do you think?" Yaz is saying. "Or maybe not. Maybe she didn't even know, because maybe

Modessa was putting on an act for her. Like, maybe Modessa thought it would be fun to..."

Yaz talks and talks. Katie-Rose shifts positions on the sofa and sighs, thinking about how Yaz's voice sounds different over the phone than it does in person. Most people's do, but Yaz's does more so than others. Maybe because Yaz is already so soft-spoken, even when she's feeling urgent about something or other? Maybe the *whisper-shush* of the phone lines—if phone lines even exist anymore (do they?)—wrap around Yaz's words and cloak them in one extra layer of telephone gossamer, muffling them just a snitch, just enough to make them buzz in Katie-Rose's head?

She has had enough of the buzz, she decides.

"*SO!*" she says, loudly and brightly.

Yasaman stops in the middle of her sentence. "Um... huh?"

Katie-Rose plasters a wide smile on her face, because even if a person can't see your expression, she can hear it, and if you're smiling, you sound smiley. And Katie-Rose needs to sound smiley in order to lure Yaz away from the non-smiliness of all things Modessa.

"Have you found any stray bubble-gum balls in your basement?" Katie-Rose asks. "From the bubble-gum treasure hunt?"

"Um, I haven't looked. I got home and called you straightaway."

"Ahhh. Well, you probably should make a sweep of the basement just in case, because you don't want your mom or dad tripping over a rogue bubble-gum ball and falling on their heads or anything."

"Why would they fall on their heads?"

"Because bubble-gum balls are balls! Round! Slippery! Like banana peels, only worse. Like marbles, only worse!"

"Oh," Yaz says. "You're right. Maybe I should go check ..."

"And Nigar. Is she back to being Nigar, or is she still Princess Bubblelina?"

Yaz laughs, an excellent sign. "At home? Nigar. At school? Lucy was calling Nigar 'Princess Bubblelina,' and Nigar was calling Lucy 'Lucilicious.'"

"She's living two lives," Katie-Rose says approvingly. "I like it!"

"You are so strange, Katie-Rose," Yaz says. "My little sister is not living two lives, and I don't even know what that means, and why would you want her to, anyway?"

That question sets a new course for the conversation, and the two girls argue (in a friendly way) about whether a girl could live two lives, or whether she'd get caught eventually. Also about whether a girl can change over time—like, really change, and not just change the color of her hair or whether she wears all black or whatever—or if you are who you are and that's that, the end.

All in all, Katie-Rose is quite pleased with herself for successfully distracting Yaz from the Medusa Wars saga. She doesn't know how long it'll last, however, so she signs off while their convo's on a high point.

"Adios, dahling. See you tomorrow," she says.

"Adios to you," Yaz says. "Bye."

Katie-Rose clicks the "off" button and rests the phone against her chest. Disaster—or drama—averted.

Tuesday, November 15

camilla

Milla borrows her Mom Abigail's iPhone and texts Max, who is both a boy and her friend, and who is even her semi-boyfriend. Okay, her real live boyfriend, if she's being totally honest and not blushingly embarrassed. Max is her boyfriend, and Milla is Max's girlfriend, and the reason she knows this is because she knows her heart well enough to be able to say, *Yes, this is something, and it's not one-sided. It's both-sided. We like each other, Max and I, and . . . yay!!!!*

What Milla *doesn't* know is what it means, exactly, to be in the fifth grade and have a boyfriend. Should she hold his hand one day? Kiss him? No way, too scary. (But what if he kisses her, or tries to? *Eeek!*)

For now? Texting is enough. It's super a lot of fun, especially with all the emoji that can be added to the texts. Big happy grins! Hearts! Octopi! Strange balls of food on sticks!

Oh, and Max has *his very own iPhone*, that lucky boy. He calls it his "portable computer that has phone functionality built in." Tee-hee, so adorkable.

Max! Wassup?

Hi, Milla. I was just thking about u. Well, u and C++.

C++? U got a C++ on something? What?????

No it's a computer lnauge.

Language. Sorry.

A computer language? What do u do with it?

C++? Anywhing!

Anywhing?

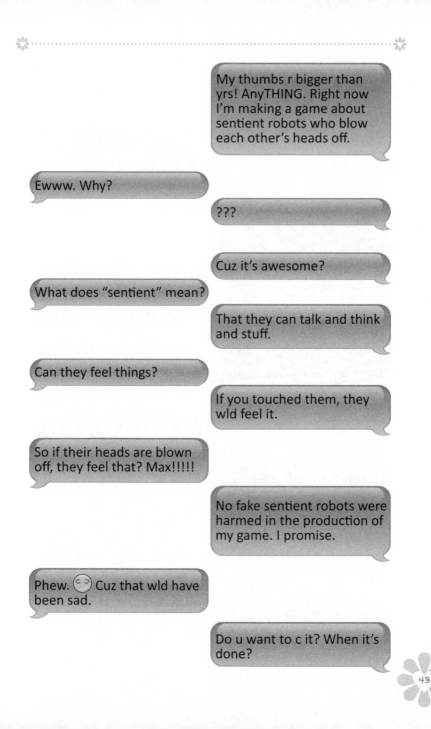

The robot killing game? Uh . . . sure?

You can help me name it. It'll be beta for a while, but when it goes live, it'll need a REALLY good name.

What does "beta" mean? nvm, it's prolly some geeky thing, right? I already have a really good name for it. Wanna hear?

U kidding? YEAH!!!!

"The Happy Game of Happy Unicorns and Starflowers, in Which No One Dies or Gets His Head Blown Off."

Thats a terrible name. No officne.

No *officne* taken, tee-hee. Especially cuz that's a great name!!!! If I saw a game like that, I wld play it in a heartbeat.

No

now I AM offended.

+huffs+

U r?

No, u silly! I'm KIDDING!!!!

Oh. Pew!

I mean PHEW!!!!!

Yr so weird!

gtg—my mom sez time for school.

but, Milla?

Yes, Max?

well, I was wondering . . .

Yes, Max???

U don't have to. Obviously. But do u maybe wanna go out for s and ? Um, with me?

Our parents cld come too. That's what my mom said. But we cld go to Olive Garden and we cld sit at one table and they cld sit at another.

Only Olive Garden dsn't serve s, I don't think.

They do, actually. They're mainly famous for pasta, but they have hamburgers 2.

There isn't a pizza emoji, that's all.

That's ok.

Yeah, but that's why I put a hamburger. But, so do u? Want to do that, maybe?

Oh! I have to ask my moms. I mean, I want to, but I have to get permission.

ok

I'll ask and report back, k?

Yeah. I hope they say yes!

I'm going to school now. Bye!

Milla's Mom Abigail is calling Milla, too. Milla's been pretending that she didn't hear, but now she wanders into the kitchen and gives Mom Abigail her phone back—*after* carefully deleting all the texts between her and Max.

"Okeydoke, Mill-the-Pill," Mom Abigail says. "Homework? Lunch? Do you have everything you need before heading to the car?"

"Yes, ma'am, Mom-ma'am," Milla says.

Her mom smiles and tousles her hair. "Great. So who were you talking to just now?"

"No one. Max. But we weren't talking. We were texting."

"Ah," her mom says. She likes Max. Everyone likes Max. "Anything exciting going on?"

"No, not really. He, um, gave me the weather report, that's all." He didn't, but Milla isn't ready to bring up the Olive Garden yet. "It's going to be on the chilly side, so you better take a jacket, because don't you have that picnic thing today?"

Milla's Mom Abigail is a caterer, and last night she told Milla and Milla's Mom Joyce about a "Cupcakes, Coffee, and Koi" event that's she's throwing this morning. The lady who hired Mom Abigail wants the food served in her backyard even though it's November, because she has a new fishpond she wants to show off. Hence the "Cupcakes, Coffee, and *Koi*" theme (though the koi will not be served as food).

"I do," Mom Abigail says. "Hey, thanks for the reminder."

"I'll go get your cute pink jacket," Milla says. "That fluffy marshmallow one."

She skips off to the coat closet. Pizza! Burgers! Maybe ice cream, and *definitely* Max!

First she'll tell her besties. Yaz will be wide-eyed and full of awe. Katie-Rose will either scowl *or* tease her and make smoochie-smoochie sounds. As for Violet, she'll help Milla pick out the perfect-o outfit, cute and chic and just exactly right.

Except, wait. She stops skipping all at once, realizing that if she tells her FFFs, then that makes her date with Max *real*. If it even is a "date." Is it a date?

Maybe she won't tell her besties about the . . . whatever-it-is that Max has suggested quite yet after all. Eventually she will, of course!

Well, probably.

Maybe.

But honestly, it makes more sense to find out more from Max about when he's imagining this . . . thing . . . will actually happen. Then she'll check in with her moms, who might say "yes" but might say "no." If they say "no," there's not much reason to tell her besties anyway, is there?

But if they say "yes"...?

Milla shivers.

It will be epic.

Six

It's the beginning of the school day, but Ms. Perez hasn't started teaching yet. She's doing that sneaky-teacher move called freewriting, where the kids in the class are supposed to work on their writing assignment for the week while Ms. Perez finishes her cup of coffee. Hardly anyone but Yaz does the assignment, though, so instead of "freewriting time," it's more like free time, period, which kids use in a variety of different ways:

- Some write notes to their friends. Medusa and Quin are big note writers, big surprise. Their notes are no doubt mean, because there is always a lot of sniggering when they pass them back and forth.

- Elena used to stare out the window, probably daydreaming about horses, but now she has joined the note-passing ranks with Medusa and Quin.

- Chance, who claims he has fifteen different girlfriends in fifteen different states, draws cartoon strips. Katie-Rose has seen Chance's cartoons. They're not bad. Nevertheless, she is highly doubtful of his girlfriend collection.

- Natalia Totenburg also uses the time to draw. She alternates between poking her enormous headgear with her eraser and drawing detailed pictures of cheerleaders. Natalia's pictures are good, too, but cheerleaders? Why?!

- As for the rest of the kids in the class, it's anyone's guess what they're up to. Some, like Yasaman, are hunched over their journals, but Katie-Rose would bet dollars to doughnuts that most of them are scribbling stuff like, "Here I am writing. Just writing. Writing anything at all, that's what I'm doing, la la la." When Ms. Perez makes her occasional classroom scan, that's the sort of gibberish Katie-Rose writes, anyway.

Ms. Perez seems particularly tuned out this morning, however, and Katie-Rose would never admit it, but she's bored with no actual work to do. To pass the time, she props her elbows on her desk and her chin in her palms and beams her laser-like eyeball energy at a boy two rows in front of her. His name is Preston, and he is annoying, but also slightly cute (in an annoying way). Not that she would ever ever EVER in a squillion years admit such a thing.

"Preston, Preston, Preston," Katie-Rose says under her breath. She uses a menacing voice, because it is entertaining. Come to think of it, maybe Preston is only (slightly) cute because although he is unquestionably annoying, he is easy *to* annoy. And annoying Preston is one of life's great pleasures.

He lifts his head, looks straight at her, and catches her staring. He *winks* at her, and she jerks back and almost topples over in her chair.

He chuckles, and she narrows her eyes.

"You think that's funny?" Katie-Rose says under her

breath. She continues addressing him, but in her head: *You almost killed me, and you think it's funny? Well, hardy har har har har, you're soooooooo hysterical. You should join the circus, or better yet, clown school. Why don't you join clown school, Preston, huh?*

Preston lounges in his chair, grinning insolently and twirling his pen between his fingers. He's wearing white skinny jeans (it takes an exceedingly confident boy to pull off white skinny jeans, she'll give him that) and a blue shirt that has a velvet snake-like pattern on it.

Skater-dude hip, that's his vibe. Katie-Rose's gaze travels upward, and she notices that he even has—

Whoa!

"Preston!" she whisper-hisses.

"Yes, She Who Adoreth Me?"

She waves that off with an irritable finger-flutter. "Preston—you got your *ear* pierced!"

"Yup, to add to my hotness factor."

"Ew," Katie-Rose says. Fifth graders are not supposed to be hot, or even say that word.

"I've got passion in my pants and I ain't afraid to show it, show it, show it," Preston croons. He waggles his eyebrows. "I'm sexy and I know it."

"Uh, no, you're disgusting," Katie-Rose says. She edges out of her desk. "But your ear. Can I see?"

"Come forth," he says. "Admire."

Katie-Rose glances at Ms. Perez, then slinks two rows forward to Preston's desk, squat-walking to keep her head at the same height as the rest of the students' heads.

"You walk like a duck," Preston comments.

Katie-Rose scowls and tries to think of a comeback.

"It's cute," he says.

She closes her mouth. Did he just say she was *cute*? Is it possible that while she was going about the morning thinking Preston was (slightly) cute, Preston was thinking the same thing about her?

Or—more likely—is he messing with her mind?

"Yeah, whatever," she says. She grabs the hair at the nape of his neck (it's surprisingly soft) and pulls him toward her, angling his head so that his pierced ear is directly in her line of vision. Jammed through his earlobe is a gunmetal-gray earring, but not an *earring* earring. Not a girly one, that is. Preston's earring is a small hoop with a ball-bearing sort of thing at the bottom. Very very *boy*.

"Whoa, that's awesome," she tells him.

"Thanks," he says. He plays it cool, but he blushes a little.

"Did you go to Claire's?" she asks, since Claire's is the store where girls almost always go to get their ears pierced.

"Claire's?" he says incredulously. "Uh . . . *no*. At Claire's, they make you hold a teddy bear so you won't be scared."

"They do?"

"That's what they did with my little sister," he says. "If you ever get your ears pierced, you'll see for yourself. You'll get to hold a cuddly widdle teddy bear, and if you want them to, they'll even take a picture for you."

"No, thank you," Katie-Rose says, which makes Preston laugh. "So if you didn't go to Claire's, where did you go?"

"I did it myself," Preston says.

Katie-Rose huffs. "Liar pants. You did not."

"Did so. Took a needle out of my mom's sewing basket and popped it right through. It really did *pop*, too." He lowers his voice, as if making sure no spies are listening. "The earlobe is a fleshy thing. There's more going on there than you'd think. You probably would have fainted."

"Uh, no," Katie-Rose says. She doesn't know whether she believes him, but she does know that she can't let him get the upper hand. "This girl does *not* faint." Unfortunately, she wobbles as she says this. She grabs his desk to keep her balance, and he grins that cocky grin.

"Do you always refer to yourself in the third person?"

"I am not about to faint, so shut up!" she hisses.

"It could be my extreme hotness," Preston muses. "Girls faint all the time when they see me. They drop like flies."

Really? Katie-Rose thinks. *Really?!!* She steals another peek at Ms. Perez—she's still grading, or Facebooking, or whatever it is she's up to—and says in her most menacing tone yet, "Preston? You. Are. Ten."

"Eleven," he corrects her.

She's momentarily thrown. He's eleven? A whole year older than she is? How did she not know that? Then she reminds herself that she doesn't care.

"Okay, *eleven*," she says. "Whoopie-dee-do. But guess what? Eleven-year-olds are not . . ." She swallows. "You can*not* say that you're . . ."

"Hot?" Preston says. He extends his leg into the aisle.

His sneaker is enormous, and when he nudges her shin, she topples onto her bottom.

"Ow!" she cries. Ms. Perez glances up. Natalia gawks, and Modessa and Quin swivel their heads in unison to see what's going on. They look at Katie-Rose, then at each other. Modessa laughs and holds her palm up so that Quin can give her a high five. Laughter spreads around the classroom. Katie-Rose feels her face heat up.

"Katie-Rose?" Yaz says anxiously. Katie-Rose is certain that Yaz is the only person in the room who cares that she fell. Everyone else just thinks it's hilarious.

"Here," Preston says, reaching to help her up. He isn't laughing, she notices. He almost looks concerned.

But Katie-Rose feels a rush of anger anyway. She pushes him away. "Leave me alone," she snaps.

"Katie-Rose . . ."

"I *said* leave me alone."

He furrows his brow. "*O-o-okay*. You're, uh, kind of prickly, aren't you?"

"Shut up, Preston. Just shut up."

He lowers his voice. "I didn't mean to make you fall."

"Well, good, because you didn't. I fell all by myself."

She blinks back tears. "You think the whole world revolves around you, Preston. But guess what? Nobody cares what you do, especially not me."

Hurt flickers across Preston's face, and Katie-Rose feels ashamed. Then just like that, his expression changes, and Katie-Rose wonders if the hurt was ever there at all.

"Down, girl," he says loudly, to the room. He holds out his hands, palms forward, as if she's a crazy dog sprawled on the floor in front of him. "I'd give you a Scooby snack, but I'm fresh out. Sorry."

The kids who were already laughing laugh harder, while those who weren't join in.

"People," Ms. Perez scolds.

Katie-Rose picks herself up off the floor and returns to her seat. Her insides are quivering, and she wonders how she ever, even for an instant, thought that Preston was (slightly) cute.

He's not, and he never will be, and if she's crazy—which she's not, but that's how he made her feel—then it's for thinking even for a minute that she liked him.

Because she doesn't, and she doesn't like his earring, either. It's stupid, and so is Preston. And she hates him.

Seven

Yasaman

asaman, could you come here, please?" Ms.
Perez asks.

"Um, yeah," Yaz says, distracted. She shakes her head
to clear it. "I mean, yes, ma'am." She glances at Katie-Rose
as she rises from her desk, but Katie-Rose won't meet her
eyes, or anyone's. Katie-Rose is a scowl in the shape of a
girl. Or a girl in the shape of a scowl? Preston just embarrassed her, and now Katie-Rose is hunched over her
notebook, scrawling away like a madman. Or a mad girl.
Her body is tiny. Her spine is curved. Fury radiates from
her like scary blue sparks of electricity.

Yaz goes to the front of the room. "Do you need help with something?" she asks Ms. Perez. Yaz is kind of like Ms. Perez's teacher's assistant, an arrangement that suits them both. "Do you want me to grade yesterday's math quizzes?"

"Thanks, sweetie," Ms. Perez says. "But I need you to deliver another note for me. Can you do that?"

"Of course," Yaz says. "To Mr. Emerson again?"

Ms. Perez blushes, which Yaz finds *extremely* interesting.

"Ah . . . yes," Ms. Perez says. She lowers her voice. "To Mr. Emerson. Right."

Yaz lowers her voice to match her teacher's. "Okay. You look really pretty today, by the way."

Ms. Perez's blush deepens.

"What? You do," Yaz says, indicating Ms. Perez's crisp white blouse with shiny silver buttons. The top two buttons are unbuttoned, and Yaz catches a glimpse of . . . um . . . the fact that her teacher has a figure that is hugely different than a ten-year-old's.

Yaz feels guilty for peeking and immediately looks away. She hopes Ms. Perez didn't notice.

"Well, that's nice of you to say," Ms. Perez says, attempting a businesswoman tone. "You look lovely yourself. And here's this."

She hands Yaz a note, which, like yesterday's, is folded over four times, making it roughly the size of a pack of gum. Ms. Perez doesn't let go of the note after Yasaman grasps it, however, so for a few seconds they hold the note together. Suspended between them, it makes Yasaman think of a bridge. *A bridge to what?* she wonders.

Finally, Ms. Perez releases the note. "Be sure to come right back!" she calls as Yaz heads out of the room.

The air in the hall feels fresher, more open, and Yasaman enjoys herself as she strolls past the water fountain, the snack cabinet, the preschool rooms. The walls outside the preschool classrooms are bright and cheerful, plastered with taped-up art projects depicting sprawling rainbows and kitty cats and stick figures with round heads and crazy-big eyes. The girl stick figures wear triangle dresses; the boys wear rectangle pants and block-shaped shirts. Yaz scans the names on the bottom of each drawing, looking for one made by Nigar.

Ooo, there! Yaz smiles. To the left of Nigar's preschool classroom is a piece of pink construction paper. Pink is Nigar's favorite color. At the top of the paper is the title of Nigar's drawing: <u>I Am Grateful for Many Things!</u> This was obviously written by Nigar's teacher, as Nigar has barely learned her alphabet, and the only words she can spell are "Nigar," "cat," and, disturbingly, "Justin Bieber." Beneath the title are a wobbling tower of line drawings, each drawing labeled by the teacher because that's the way it works in preschool.

The base of the tower consists of four jelly-bean shapes with pokey-fingered arms and pokey-toed legs jutting out of them. The jelly-bean shapes are arranged in order of size, and the third-shortest jelly bean has long hair covered by what Yasaman knows is supposed to be a *hijab*, though it looks more like a doughnut with curtains.

It's me! Yaz thinks happily.

The smallest jelly bean is Nigar. She's drawn herself with her hair in doggy ears, each doggy ear embellished with a cute hair bow. Hair bows are Nigar's trademark, according to Nigar.

Next to the clump of jelly-bean people, Nigar's teacher has penned the words "My Family." It's beautiful. It's beautiful, and it's true, and Yasaman hopes Nigar will hold on to that trueness inside of her forever. Knowing who she is. Not being afraid to share it with the world.

Yaz peeks inside Nigar's classroom but doesn't spot Nigar. She's probably over by the cage of the class hamster. She used to hate that hamster, but recently she's grown fond of him, mainly because she likes to watch him nibble lettuce.

Yasaman keeps walking. When she arrives at Mr. Emerson's room, she raps lightly on the open door and then steps inside. Milla and Violet see her, and Yaz wiggles her fingers at them. Milla waves back. Violet smiles at her.

Yaz notices the girl in the desk beside Violet's: It's the new girl. Hayley. Her body language ... She looks aloof, as if she couldn't care less what anyone thinks of her. And yet there's something that makes Yaz wonder if the aloofness is just an act. Or not. Maybe Yaz is seeing what she wants to see because she hates the thought of anyone being alone, regardless of whether the aloneness is on purpose.

She forces herself out of her trance and goes to Mr. Emerson's desk.

"From Ms. Perez," she whispers. She nods to say, *Okay? Note delivered, mission accomplished?*

"Ah-ha," Mr. Emerson says. He unfolds the note. "Why, thank you, Yasaman."

"You're welcome."

She moves to go, but he stops her, saying, "Hold up, tiger."

Tiger? Yaz thinks. But she turns around.

"The ambrosial musings of a lady most enchanting," he murmurs.

"I'm sorry . . . what?"

He doesn't respond. His eyes move over the note. Then he grins at Yasaman, and Yasaman has a fleeting image of what he might have been like as a boy. Like Preston, maybe, but not quite as annoying. Hopefully.

"Allow me a moment to inscribe a communiqué in return, hmm?" Mr. Emerson asks. Except he's not really asking. He's telling. He smacks a fresh piece of paper on his desk, sets a rock on the top left corner to hold it down, and scribbles away. Yaz is surprised by the rock until she takes the time to think about it. When Yaz writes, she steadies her paper with her left forearm. But if she didn't have a left forearm...?

Well, there you have it.

Mr. Emerson is humming by the time he finishes his communiqué, which he signs with a flourish. Yaz is dying to know *how* he signed it—John? Mr. Emerson? Yours forever?—but he folds it in half before she can see. Then half, and half, and half again. Four times he folds his note, just like Ms. Perez.

They're note-folding twins, Yaz thinks.

Mr. Emerson hands her the compact rectangle of paper. "Thar she blows," he proclaims, "and a mighty vessel she is, too!"

Yaz doesn't know what to make of his remark. Is he saying that Ms. Perez is a vessel? And not just any vessel, but a mighty one at that? He better not be.

"Off you go, slugabed," he says, shooing Yaz away.

"Can't stay in my classroom all day, although I under-stand the appeal."

Yaz returns to her classroom feeling both mystified and muddy-headed. She wants very much to read Mr. Emerson's note, but she is Yasaman, so she doesn't.

Eight

Violet

It would be nice not to care about people. You wouldn't get anxious when they were having a hard time, you wouldn't cry when they cried, you wouldn't get an upset stomach wondering if the way a person looked on the outside—tough or vulnerable, happy or sad—matched the way she actually felt on the inside.

Then again . . .

You wouldn't get to laugh so hard you almost peed when your friend reached over out of the blue to pluck from your nose what you suspect was a nonexistent nose hair. You couldn't bask in the sun and just be warmed by the company of your bestie even if you and she were simply being quiet together.

If you had no one's back, then no one would have your back.

If you cared about no one, no one would care about you.

You would know nothing of love.

And there it is: Violet's fatal flaw. She does care about others, and so she has to swallow the good and the bad that comes with it.

Her notebook is open on her desk. Her purple pen is ready at the go. She's supposed to be working on her "Where I'm From" poem, but her mind is spinning in a different direction, and if she put her thoughts on paper, here is what she would write:

When I was the new kid at Rivendell, sometimes I felt invisible. Other times, I felt too visible. And I don't know what was going on with me, but I did bad things. I wasn't my best self, and sometimes I was ... cruel ... and Modessa somehow helped that cruelty come out. It was still my fault.

I can't blame Modessa, because I knew better. But Modessa played a role, and I let her.

Why? What was wrong with me?

If someone had come right up and warned me that doing anything with Modessa would make my life worse, would I have listened?

She sighs.

She's thinking about all of this because of Hayley, of course. Yaz told her that Modessa is probably going to try to make Hayley be one of her stupid Evil Chicks, and Violet knows deep inside that even if she doesn't want to get involved, she kind of has to. If she doesn't, how could she live with herself and feel proud to be a flower friend and all that?

She rises from her desk. Mr. Emerson doesn't notice (or doesn't care—he pretty much runs a do-what-you-want classroom), but Cyril Remkiwicz does. His expression is impassive, though she knows his insides aren't. It's another reminder of how people's insides and outsides match far less often than you might think, because Violet knows that Cyril both notices and cares what Violet does, practically always. Not in a bad way.

She shoots him a small smile, which he doesn't return, because he's Cyril. The corner of his mouth slants almost imperceptibly upward, however, and his almost-smile cheers her up. For Cyril, an almost-smile is pretty good. It's a reminder that hearts *can* unclench.

She squats by Hayley, resting her hand on Hayley's desk. It's time she gave this a second try.

"Hi," she says. "How's it going?"

Hayley tilts her head, her expression as inscrutable as Cyril's. *Oh, great*, Violet thinks. *Why did I bother?*

Then, *bam*, Hayley grins, making Violet think of a piece of sucking candy that suddenly reaches its bursting point, squirting out sweet strawberry-flavored syrup.

Violet grins back. Something passes between the two girls.

"Oh, I don't know," Hayley says. "Good enough, I guess. You?"

Violet considers. "I'm good, too."

"Good!" Hayley replies. "Double good!"

Double good. Hayley's phrase latches hold in Violet's mind, and Violet's spirits lighten. She's glad she came over to Hayley. She's glad she gave her a second chance, and she surprises herself by wondering if there is a flower somewhere in the world called a "Hayley." Or if Hayley's middle name might be a flower name, like . . . Chrysanthemum? *Ha.* Or Petunia. Hayley Petunia. Not the most beautiful of names, but funny, and sometimes being funny is even better than being beautiful.

"What are you smiling about?" Hayley asks.

"Am I smiling?" Violet says. "Oh, sorry. I mean, not *sorry*, but . . ." She gives an awkward laugh. "No idea. Guess I just spaced out for a sec."

"I hear you. I do that all the time, and my uncle gets *so* mad." Hayley leans closer. "He used to be a marine. Although he says he still *is* a marine, because once a marine, always a marine. Anyway, he's way strict. *Semper fi* and all that."

"'Semper fi'? What's that?"

"The marine motto. He has it tattooed on his biceps."

"What does it mean?"

Hayley scowls. "'Eat your vegetables! Get off the phone! Pay attention, young lady, or I will whip you!'" She smooths out her expression. "That's not an exact translation, but pretty much."

"Ugh," Violet says. She checks to make sure they're still flying under Mr. Emerson's radar. He's at the whiteboard, his back toward them as he scrawls out the day's homework menu with a fat, squeaky marker.

"But why does your uncle care if you eat your vegetables or whatever?" she asks. Then she realizes how wrong that sounds. "I mean, that's good that he cares. I guess. But is he over at your house all the time or something?"

"I'm over at *his* house all the time," Hayley explains. "I live with him. *Not* my choice."

"Oh. Just with him, or is your aunt there, too? Do they have kids of their own?"

Hayley scooches over on her chair and tugs Violet up so that Violet can sit next to her. It's a tight fit and their thighs touch, but whatever. She's allowed to share Hayley's seat for a minute. It's not against the law.

"No aunt. No cousins. Just my uncle. I have to do four hours of chores before I can watch any TV, and every weekend he drags me on a thousand-mile hike because he says it builds character. Can you say 'fun'?"

Violet snorts. She's had her share of family problems; her mom had a l-o-n-g stay in the hospital recently because she felt anxious all the time and didn't know how to deal with it. But her mom's doing so much better now. *So* much better.

"Well, is your uncle *sometimes* nice?" she asks Hayley.

Hayley shrugs. "Yes. No. Maybe." She exhales. "He has a coin collection he's always wanting to show me. Does that count as nice?"

Violet isn't sure. "Is it a cool coin collection?"

Hayley eyeballs her. "They're *coins*. Little pieces of metal." She adopts the scowly voice that Violet now knows is her imitation of her uncle. "Here we have a Memorial Lincoln Cent, dated nineteen fifty-eight. Most people would call this a 'wheat penny'. They would be wrong."

Violet covers her smile with her hand.

"I know, right?" Hayley says.

"Violet and Hayley?" Mr. Emerson says.

Uh-oh.

"Um, yes?" Violet says.

"Is there a reason you're both sitting in one desk? Have you become conjoined?"

"No, not conjoined," Violet says. Hayley ducks her head. A laugh squeaks out.

"Excellent," Mr. Emerson says. "In that case, head back to your own desk, please, Violet."

Violet does as she's told, even though she has tons more questions for Hayley. Like, *why* is she living with her uncle and not her parents? Are her parents alive? (Gosh, she hopes so. How awful if they aren't!) And why did Hayley start attending Rivendell yesterday, instead of at the beginning of the year?

Violet has never known anyone with a screwier family life than her own, or at least not until Hayley, and she isn't quite sure how she feels about it. She's slightly thrilled, but she's also slightly . . . freaked out? Unnerved? *Something.*

She definitely relates, though. Sad is sad, no matter how you cut it.

Nine

Camilla

	Chat with Yasaman
MarshMilla:	Yaz! YAY!!!! I thought since it's almost 8:00, u might not be online.
Yasaman:	the 8:00 rule is more for being on the phone.
Yasaman:	but yes! yay! I'm glad u IMd, cuz I wanted to chat.
Yasaman:	hi!
MarshMilla:	hi!!!! what's up?
Yasaman:	not much. full, cuz I ate waaaaay too much pizza—my mom let us order in PIZZA! can

u believe it????—but other than that, just hanging out.

MarshMilla: me too, minus the pizza. my Mom Abigail made a fancy chicken dish, only she didn't call it chicken. She called it poo-lay.

Yasaman: ooo la la!

Yasaman: hey . . . so what do you think about the new girl? Hayley?

MarshMilla: hmmm. GOOD QUESTION.

MarshMilla: I don't know her well enough to say . . .

MarshMilla: I tried smiling at her in class, but she didn't smile back. She'll smile at Violet, but not me.

Yasaman: that's weird

MarshMilla: yeah . . . it IS, isn't it? I thought so, too.

MarshMilla: but I didn't want to say anything. I mean, we shld give her a chance and all that.

Yasaman: she does seem to like Violet. Hayley, I mean. and Violet seems to like her back.

MarshMilla: +shrugs+

MarshMilla: katie-rose thinks Hayley is being *too* nice to Violet—she told me so during

break. or maybe she secretly thinks Violet
is being too nice to Hayley?

MarshMilla: I think k-r just doesn't like outsiders, no
matter who they are. that she wants the
four of us to stay the four of us, end of
story.

Yasaman: **but you're okay with it? with Hayley?**

MarshMilla: well, I told Violet to ask her to eat with
us tomorrow, didn't I? we have enuff
flower love to share with Hayley for 1
lunch. Heck, same for Elena, IF she ever
decides to come back from THE DARK
SIDE. +spooky fingers+ +ghostie sounds+
oooo-oooo!

Yasaman: **I need to make a ghostie smilie for our site!!!**

Yasaman: **but since I haven't, how about instead of
oooo-ooooo, u can say *moooo-oooo!***

MarshMilla: u make me laff, yaz. I love that fat little
cow. I also love the new elephant smilie.

Yasaman: **U make me laff, too.**

Yasaman:	**and I like how u put in 4 elephants, 1 for each of us.**
MarshMilla:	cuz elephants never forget, and WE will never forget, either. we'll never forget about our flower power, so k-r really doesn't need to worry about Violet and Hayley. that's what *I* think.
Yasaman:	**I agree!**
MarshMilla:	so . . . can I tell u something?
Yasaman:	**of course. Is it about elephants? Is it elephantilicious?**
MarshMilla:	erm . . . elephantilicious isn't *exactly* the word I'd use . . .
Yasaman:	**then what word wld you use? Spill!**
MarshMilla:	now I'm nervous.
MarshMilla:	I know. I'll give u a multiple-choice test, and you can guess. K?
MarshMilla:	Do u think the thing I want to tell you about is a) scary, b) exciting, c) tummy-twisty, or . . . um . . . d) romantic?
Yasaman:	**romantic! romantic!**
Yasaman:	**so I pick D! Romantic! *And* B, exciting! But**

that means it's about Max. Am I right? And if it's about Max, I cld see how it might be scary and tummy-twisty, too.

Yasaman: can I pick E? As in all of the above????

MarshMilla: yes. I guess.

MarshMilla: eeeek!

Yasaman: okay, but tell me more! What is the scary-exciting-tummy-twisty-romantic thing that is making Milla the Mousie go *eeek*?!!

MarshMilla: *big breath*

MarshMilla: HE ASKED ME TO GO TO THE OLIVE GARDEN WITH HIM!

MarshMilla: omg, typing that out makes it seem REAL. omg, way too freaky.

MarshMilla: but do you understand the *eeek* now?

Yasaman: eeek-eeek squeak-squeak!!!!

Yasaman: Max-Max asked you out *on a date,* Mills! WHOA!!!!

MarshMilla: NOT a date!!!!! just do I want to go to dinner with him. That is all!

Yasaman: which is called a *date,* goofball.

MarshMilla: but our parents wld be there. They'd sit

at another table, but that means it's *not* a date, right?

Yasaman: do you *want* it to not be a date? *I* think it's super a lot exciting that he asked you out, and *I* think it *is* a date!

MarshMilla: no comment

Yasaman: now if he came over to our table during lunch, held out a grape, and said, "hey, Milla, here's a grape," *that* wouldn't be a date.

MarshMilla: right, cuz it wld be a grape. ha ha. +laughs nervously+

MarshMilla: (that was me making a joke, cuz of course a grape isn't a date.) (i'm talking in this case about the kind of date you eat.) (the fruit kind.) (are dates a fruit???) (and I was being funny, cuz that was a joke.) (did you get it?)

Yasaman: dates—the eating kind—are delicious. but yr just trying to distract me, cuz we are

not talking about the eating kind of dates.
We're talking about DATE dates, even if you
don't want to call it that!

Yasaman: did you tell him yes? Plz tell me you said yes.
You said yes, right?

MarshMilla: +gulps+ +gazes out window+ +points+

MarshMilla: Look! An elephant, right here in Southern
California! 🐘

Yasaman: ENUFF WITH THE ELEPHANTS!

Yasaman: yr abusing the elephant privilege!

Yasaman: now did u tell Max yes, Mills? YOU CAN'T
LEAVE ME HANGING!

MarshMilla: well, I didn't say yes . . . but I didn't say
no, either.

MarshMilla: I told him I'd ask my moms.

Yasaman: and . . . ?

MarshMilla: he only mentioned it this morning! We
were txting before school, and he didn't
say when the date wld be. He just said
wld I like to?

Yasaman: See! YOU CALLED IT A DATE!

Yasaman:	**did you ask yr moms? If u haven't yet, I think u shld ask yr Mom Abigail first. She'll say yes for sure.**
MarshMilla:	all right, well, and here is the problem. When Max first asked me, I was super excited, too—just like you.
MarshMilla:	but then time passed, and I didn't get the chance to ask Mom Abigail, and then *more* time passed . . .
MarshMilla:	and now I'm just nervous!!!! And by the way, YOU ARE THE ONLY ONE I'VE TOLD, SO DON'T TELL THE OTHERS, K?
Yasaman:	**wait—so u left Max hanging? poor max-max!!!**
MarshMilla:	well, when you put it *that* way . . .
MarshMilla:	I don't like it when you put it that way. Wld u plz not put it that way?
Yasaman:	**then ask yr moms! U can't leave poor Max just waiting and wondering and holding his breath! He'll turn blue and explode!**
MarshMilla:	I don't want him to *explode*.

Yasaman:	then call him. Or txt him. Ask yr moms if you can go, and then give him yr answer!
MarshMilla:	but I'm scared 😳
Yasaman:	doesn't matter, and you know why?
MarshMilla:	why?
Yasaman:	cuz u have to do things *even if yr scared*. You just tell yrself, "ok, I'm scared," but then u do them anyway.
MarshMilla:	oh
Yasaman:	yup
Yasaman:	You can do this, Milla. I promise.
MarshMilla:	. . .
Yasaman:	Max was prolly scared when *he* asked *you*. Have you thought of that?
MarshMilla:	. . .
Yasaman:	ask yr moms tonight, and then txt Max yr answer.
MarshMilla:	you believe in me? For reals?
Yasaman:	for reals. And now I'm logging off, and YOU *KNOW* WHAT THAT MEANS.
Yasaman:	you can do it! good luck! be strong! LOVE YOU!!!!! 💜 🐘 💜

Wednesday, November 16

✳ Ten ✳

atie-Rose has two older brothers, Charlie and Sam. Sometimes they're dreadful, like when they call Katie-Rose "shrimp" or say, *"Leave*, Katie-Rose," when their friends are over and they're having stupid video-game bonanzas. But other times, they are the best brothers in the world. Like the time Katie-Rose, Charlie, and Sam were hanging out at their neighborhood park, and another boy called Katie-Rose a shrimp. Katie-Rose didn't even know the boy, and the boy sure didn't know her. He was just a random jerk.

The random jerk's Frisbee whacked Katie-Rose in the head, and while Katie-Rose was still reeling from the blow, he sneered and called out, "Hey, shrimp. Give me back my Frisbee."

Well. Charlie strode right over to that jerk and shoved him in the chest. Sam followed on Charlie's heels and shoved him again, for good measure.

"Dudes," the bully said, pissed and baffled. "What's your problem?"

"Shut it," Charlie said.

"Yeah," Sam said. "Don't call her that, and if you're going to come out here with your Frisbee, then learn how to throw it."

"What the . . .?" the bully said. He wore a striped rugby shirt and a face full of arrogance. He was thicker than Charlie, but Charlie was taller. He was meaner looking than Sam, but Sam's eyes were narrow and his jaw cut a sharp line in the bright sunlight.

The bully glanced from Charlie to Sam, from Sam to Charlie. "What's it to *you*?"

"She's our sister, ****head," Charlie said. (The bad word Charlie said thrilled Katie-Rose, but it was *bad* bad, so no way is she repeating it.) He shoved the bully again, and the bully faltered.

"Dude. Chill," he said, backing away with his palms out.

"Make him apologize!" Katie-Rose told Charlie, tugging on his sleeve. He shrugged her off and gave her a scornful look, as if to say, *Don't push it, squirt.* He and Sam returned to playing basketball with their buddies, and Katie-Rose watched them, her heart bursting with pride.

"Those are my brothers," she whispered.

Before school this morning, as Charlie and Sam roughhoused their way through breakfast, Sam elbowed Charlie in the ribs in order to wrest the box of Frosted Flakes from him.

"*Ow*, you ****head!" Charlie cried, dropping the Frosted Flakes onto the floor. The liner bag burst, and Frosted Flakes scattered everywhere. Snow in November! Crunchy, sugary snow!

Sam laughed triumphantly, and Charlie scowled. He went to the junk drawer by the telephone, yanked it open, and grabbed a fine-point black Sharpie. He did something mysterious with said Sharpie, turning his back to Sam (and by default to Katie-Rose) and muttering under his breath. He chucked the Sharpie into the drawer and took two big steps toward Sam, Frosted Flakes crunching beneath his oversize sneakers.

"You mess with me, you mess with this!" he said, clenching his right hand into a fist and thrusting it two inches in front of Sam's nose.

"With what? With what?" Katie-Rose said, scrambling out of her chair at the kitchen table.

Sam pushed Charlie's fist away—Charlie would never hit Sam for real, or their mom would have his hide—but not before Katie-Rose saw what Charlie had done. He'd used the Sharpie to write the letters "T," "H," "I," and "S" on his knuckles. Katie-Rose giggled helplessly. *You mess with me, you mess with THIS*, with Charlie's knuckles actually spelling out the word "this."

"Geez-o-criminy," Sam said. "And you're the older, more mature brother? Really?"

Charmed in equal measure by Charlie's THIS fist and Sam's use of "geez-o-criminy," Katie-Rose vowed then and there to use both bits of clevernesses as often as she could during the school day.

With "geez-o-criminy," she's had huge success, sprinkling the phrase into practically every sentence that comes out of her mouth. When Ms. Perez calls Yaz up front and asks her to go on yet another note-running errand, Katie-Rose mutters, "Geez-o-criminy. Enough with the notes already!" When Natalia Totenburg asks what set of math problems they're supposed to be working on, Katie-Rose flings her hands into the air. "Geez-o-criminy, Natalia!" she cries. "You expect *me* to know? What am I, a game-show host?"

The THIS fist is proving to be a tougher nut to crack. The "T," the "H," the "I," and the "S" are ready and waiting. Katie-Rose inked them onto her knuckles on the way to school. She hasn't been able to use them, however. It isn't Katie-Rose's fault. It's just that violence isn't allowed at Rivendell. Not even fake violence. Not even mock and ironic fake violence.

*I *will* find a way*, she thinks, drumming her fingers on her desk. "Mwahaha!" she says, trying to sound like a hardened criminal. And then again for good measure: "Mwaha*ha*haha!"

"Do you need a lozenge?" Natalia whispers, only it comes out *lothenge* because of her lisp.

"What?" Katie-Rose says. She glances around the room, startled to find that she's not in a smoky café at all. Nor is she dressed in all black; nor is her face cloaked in the shadow of a wide-brimmed fedora.

"A *lothenge*," Natalia repeats. "For your thore throat. Another exthellent tip ith to uthe a neti pot. Do you have a neti pot? Neti potth are awethome for loothening phlegm."

Preston turns around from his desk. He cracks up. "Yeah, Katie-Rose. For your phlegm."

Katie-Rose sticks her tongue out at him.

"I do not have phlegm," she informs Natalia.

"Then why were you clearing your throat?" Natalia asks.

"I wasn't. It was my—" She breaks off. One can't say "It was my evil laugh" to a girl like Natalia. She would never understand.

Preston now clears his throat repeatedly and with

enthusiasm. He sounds as if he's hocking up a dead frog.

"Shut it," Katie-Rose tells him.

Preston draws back as if he's scared. "Ooo. Prickly, prickly." He leans toward Natalia and pretends to be whispering to her, but it's clear his words are for Katie-Rose. "So much phlegm," he says with a sigh. "Maybe that's why she's so grumpy, do you think? *Or* . . . maybe she's so phlegmy because she's such a grump!"

Katie-Rose narrows her eyes. Natalia just looks confused.

"No," Natalia says. "Phlegm ith a liquid thecreted by our mucuth membraneth. It cometh from the lungth. It'th in the thame family as thputum, if you mutht know."

"Ah," Preston says. "Thputum. I mean, *sputum*. So Katie-Rose is full of sputum?"

"I said *shut it!*" Katie-Rose growls.

Preston grins, and Katie-Rose glares. Then she gets an idea, and *she* grins, but sneakily, keeping her grin on the inside. She clenches her hand into a fist.

"If your phlegm ith green or dark yellow, you need to thee a doctor, Katie-Rothe," Natalia says.

"Truer words were never spoken," Preston says. "Is it, Katie-Rose? Green or dark yellow?"

"Stop messing with me, Preston," Katie-Rose warns, hoping he doesn't. If only she knew how to crack her knuckles. Cracking her knuckles would be an excellent gesture to throw in about now.

"I don't think I can, because now I'm really curious," Preston says. "Let's talk about its consistency. Would you describe it as gelatinous or more like Cream of Wheat?" He waggles his eyebrows. "Or Cream of Sputum. *Mmmm.*"

All right. That's it. Katie-Rose crosses from her desk to his and says, "I *told* you to shut it, Preston, and you didn't listen, and now you have to face the music. You mess with me"—she thrusts her Sharpie-decorated fist in front of his face—"and you mess with *this!*"

Preston's brow furrows, and then clears. And then he cracks up, starting with a chuckle, which builds to a chortle, which crescendos into the full-out, desk-slapping laugh that only fifth-grade boys with the most obnoxious personalities can pull off.

"'SIHT'? You want me to mess with 'SIHT'?" he says. "I'm sorry, Katie-Rose, but I don't know what that means."

Other kids in the class turn to see what's so funny, and Katie-Rose feels her cheeks heat up. Yaz still isn't back from Mr. Emerson's room, and Katie-Rose feels very alone. She's been the kid that others have laughed at far too many times.

She tries to hold her head high. "You mess with me, you mess with *this*," she says in a low voice. She shakes her fist at him so that he can read the word. It's only four letters long. It's not that hard. "Stop trying to make me look stupid."

"Stop trying to make yourself look stupid," Preston says, pushing her fist out of his face. "Read it and weep, hotcakes."

Katie-Rose reads the word written on her hand. The word she herself wrote on her hand. She frowns, because her knuckles *do* spell "SIHT," only with an upside-down "T." "SIHⱢ."

Oh, crud. She thinks back to this morning's car ride, when she carefully sketched and darkened the letters "T,"

95

"H," "I," and "S" on her knuckles, all capitalized for easier reading. It looked right at the time, with her fingers flat on her jeans. *THIS*, her knuckles spelled, with the "T" on her pinky and the "S" on her forefinger.

But in fist form, with the fist in Preston's face . . .

She slinks to her seat, shoves her hand beneath her opposite bicep, and buries her head in her arms. Kids are still laughing. They're laughing enough that Ms. Perez is telling the class to settle down, not that anyone's listening.

"Hey," Preston says. "Katie-Rose. *Hey.*"

She ignores him. He's a jerk, just like that bully at the park, and she's an idiot for ever, ever thinking anything else.

"It's funny," Preston insists.

"You mess with me, you mess with SIHT!" Preston's friend Chance says in a gangster accent.

"Dude, shut up," Preston tells him.

"Preston!" Ms. Perez says. Judging by her tone, she's been trying to get his attention for a while. "Do I need to come back there? What is going *on?*"

"Nothing," Preston says. "Everything's cool." He drops his voice. "But geez, Katie-Rose, you really *are* prickly. Learn to take a joke, will you?"

A tear squeezes out of Katie-Rose's tightly shut eyes. *Prickly girls don't cry*, she tells herself, but it does no good. Maybe because prickly girls also lie.

Eleven

Violet

Mr. Emerson writes the word of the day on the whiteboard: *Gasser. Noun. Something that is extraordinarily pleasing or successful, especially a funny joke.* Violet smiles, knowing that Katie-Rose would find the word "gasser" particularly pleasing. "Did you hear the gasser I told Milla before class started?" she'd say, trying it out. "Hi*lar*ious. I about split my gut from laughing so hard!"

Even if Katie-Rose hadn't told Milla a gasser, she'd say that. Katie-Rose doesn't care if something's real or make-believe, just as long as it's entertaining and involves

Katie-Rose in a starring role. Oh, and one other small detail: just as long as the FFFs (and for the most part no one else) are her audience.

Katie-Rose adores her tribe of flower friends forever, and she's fiercely loyal to the friends *as a foursome*. She has little need for other people, however, and she has strong opinions about not allowing others into their circle. She's afraid they'll mess up the mix, that's what Violet thinks. But she also thinks, *Sorry, Charlie. Sometimes we all have to share.*

Mr. Emerson turns and faces his students. "Someone use 'gasser' in a sentence, please."

"That gasser was so stinky it about blew my leg off!" Thomas calls out. People laugh.

"*N-n-no*," Mr. Emerson says. "Read the definition first."

"'Don't light a match around a gasser or you'll blow your head off?" Thomas says.

Mr. Emerson pushes his hand through his hair. "Thomas. If I go to the trouble of giving you a word of the day, a glorious word of the day, then you will use that word of the day *properly*. You will rehearse and absorb and practice that word until it is part of you. Do you understand?"

"It's already part of me," Thomas says. "The gas part, anyway." He looks from student to student, egging them to laugh. "Am I right? I'm right, right?"

"Your wit delights us all," Mr. Emerson tells Thomas. "*Write down* a sentence using the word 'gasser,' everyone. On a piece of paper, using a writing utensil of your choice."

Thomas tries to speak.

"Thank you, but no," Mr. Emerson says. "Write. Your. Sentence. And after you've done that, pull out your 'Where I'm From' poems and work on those."

Kids bend over their notebooks. Violet intends to do the same, but a movement at the door catches her attention. It's Yasaman, again, hovering just inside Mr. Emerson's classroom for the third morning in a row.

Is she bringing Mr. E another note? She is. Violet can see the scrap of paper between Yaz's clenched fingers.

"Yasaman, my little flower," Mr. Emerson says. "Do you come bearing good tidings?"

Yaz shoots Violet a quick smile before going to him. While Yaz and Mr. Emerson speak in whispers, Violet quickly composes not just one but three word-of-the-day sentences, each using "gasser" in the right way:

1) Did you hear the gasser Katie-Rose told Milla? I about split my gut from laughing so hard!

2) I wonder if Yasaman thinks it's a gasser when Mr. E calls her a little flower.

3) Thomas's gassers aren't as funny as he thinks they are, but they're not totally un-funny, either.

With that out of the way, she tears a clean piece of notebook paper out of her spiral. If Mr. Emerson and Ms. Perez can pass notes in class—because that's what they're basically doing, right? With Yaz as their messenger?—then so can Violet.

She taps her chin with her pen, then scribbles this message:

Hayley—

Want to eat lunch with me today? With me and my friends?

❋ Violet (the girl sitting next to you)

She folds the note into a triangle and tosses it at

Hayley's desk. Hayley glances at it, then glances at Violet.

At the front of the room, Mr. E claps Yaz's shoulder in a wrapping-things-up sort of way. Yaz heads out, waving at Violet as she passes.

"Bye," Violet mouths.

She turns back to Hayley, but . . . *huh*. Violet's note is gone. The note is gone, and Hayley is plugging away at her sentences or her poem, one or the other. Red curls hang in front of Hayley's eyes, making it hard for Violet to see Hayley's expression.

Violet swallows. Where is the note?? Why does Violet feel so naked all of a sudden???

Hayley continues to write, but as she writes, she jerks her head in a very deliberate sort of way. A *look down, silly* sort of way.

Violet does, and her muscles relax. *There's* the note, right on top of Violet's spiral. Only it's still in its triangle shape. Did Hayley even read it?

One way to find out, she tells herself. She slides the note onto her lap and unfolds it using small, deft movements. Hayley *did* read it! She read it and wrote Violet a reply, too.

Sure, it says below Violet's lunch invitation. *Sounds fun.*

Oh. Wait.

Sounds like a GASSER, that is.

—H

A grin stretches across Violet's face. It starts off small and keeps growing.

Twelve

Oh my goodness, Yaz thinks. *Oh my goodness, oh my goodness, oh my goodness.* She stops by the water fountain and leans against the wall to catch her breath. Her heart pounds: *bam bam bam.* Her face feels flushed, and when she wipes her forehead, her fingers come away damp with sweat. All this, and she isn't even in PE!

She's in the hall, midway between Mr. Emerson's room and Ms. Perez's room, that's all.

She's on the way back from running an errand for her beloved teacher, that's all.

An errand that involved delivering a note to Mr. Emerson. Just a note from one teacher to another, that's all.

And she's a good girl—a *very* good girl—so when Mr. Emerson asked her (again!) to hold up while he penned a reply to Ms. Perez's note, she said yes, and that's all there was to that interaction. There's nothing unusual or blush-worthy about being an errand girl for her teachers. What could possibly be unusual or blush-worthy about that?

Except.

"Oh my goodness gracious," Yaz says aloud, her voice the faintest breeze stirring the air molecules around her. "What have I done?"

She sinks to the floor, sitting on her bottom with her knees pulled close. The note she's supposed to return to Ms. Perez dangles from her hand, which dangles from her wrist, which is connected to her forearm, which is propped on her knee. So many bones holding her body together, some of them big and others as small and delicate as a snail's shell.

Yaz remembers learning that there are twenty-six bones in a human foot. Surely there are as many (if not more!) in a human hand. It's mind-boggling. And if there are twenty-six or more bones in a human hand, then how many bones are in an entire human body? Add in a second human, then a third, then a classroom full of humans, a city full of humans, a *continent* full of humans . . .

And bones are only one piece of the puzzle! There are tendons to consider, too, and joints and muscles and skin and . . . and . . . *ligaments*, and every single part of a person's body matters when it comes to holding that body together.

Same goes for friendships. Same goes for families. Same goes for communities and neighborhoods and congregations and *jemaahs*, which are the equivalent of congregations, basically, but for mosques instead of churches. So much goes into holding any relationship together, whatever the relationship's particular flavor is.

Yaz thinks it's amazing and beautiful and glorious that relationships exist, period. The fact that they're complicated doesn't matter one bit. That's just the way relationships work, especially new relationships. And a new relationship, an early-days relationship that's just starting to bloom . . . oh, it's *so* amazing and beautiful and glorious!

That's why she read the note. That's all. Not to be sneaky or devious or *bad*.

So why is her heart thumping so crazily? Why is sweat dotting her hairline, right where her *hijab* meets her skin?

Oh my goodness gracious with gravy on top, she thinks. She is not equipped for a life of crime, that's for sure. She'd die from the stress of it. She might die right now. Or if she doesn't die, she might at least faint.

Katie-Rose would be so jealous if she fainted. No, not jealous, but mad. She'd be like, "Really, Yaz? You just had to faint right that second, with not a single soul watching? You couldn't have waited until I was there to film you? REALLY????"

Yaz presses the back of her head against the painted brick wall. She closes her eyes, but she doesn't faint. Instead, she breathes. In—one, two, three—and out. In—one, two, three—and out. She breathes and tells herself to calm down and tries to think.

You are not trapped at the bottom of a coal mine, she reminds herself. *You are not being eaten by a wild lion that escaped from the zoo. You read an itsy-bitsy note*

passed between two teachers, that's all. An itsy-bitsy note
THAT HAPPENED TO BE A LOVE LETTER (!!!), that's all!

She *could* drop the note. She could. She could separate her thumb and forefinger, and *floof*! The note would flutter to the ground, graceful as a butterfly.

Or she could read it again. Why not, given that she already has?

Oh my goodness, she thinks for the fourth or seventh or forty-ninth time. What would the Imam at her mosque say? Doing a bad thing is, obviously, bad. But if she's already done the bad thing . . .

Well, doing it once is bad. Is doing it two times twice as bad?

Out of the blue, she remembers her sister's poem, the one on the wall. The one that said, "Look at me. I am sweet and honest and don't hide things." Yaz was—is—proud of Nigar for being like that, and she thought she was that way, too.

Turns out she's not, because *look*: There go her hands, her very own hands, unfolding the note again. And now her eyeballs, her very own eyeballs, travel over her teachers' love letter for the second time, starting with Ms. Perez's initial message to Mr. Emerson.

Hey there, my hottie-with-a-body, Yaz reads, and her pulse accelerates all over again. Because "hottie-with-a-body"? *Hottie-with-a-body?!* From her *teacher* to her *other teacher*?!!

Okay. Stop freaking out, Yaz commands herself.

She tries again:

Hey there, my hottie-with-a-body. I'm having my kids study their vocab while I pretend to write tomorrow's quiz questions, but oh dear, I'm actually writing you, aren't I?

I'm a devil. I know. But is it my fault you're so cute?

Sure did have fun last night. Hope you did, too.

When do I get to see you again? Other than in the halls or the teachers' lounge, I mean. It's been less than twelve hours, and I miss you already! I miss your kisses. You're an excellent kisser, Mr. Teacher Sir.

Yours,
Maria

Ah, Maria. Maria, Maria, Maria. I love saying your name—can you tell? Even if I'm writing it, I love it just the same. And I'm fairly certain you know how much I enjoyed our evening, too. I'm fairly certain you know that "fun" doesn't come close to describing how magical it was, in so many ways. (And fine, fine, I'll admit it once again: though the magic of the evening had little to do with your Magic Cookie Bars, the cookies (bars?) were indeed delicious, the coconut notwithstanding.)

You have converted me, Maria.

I am a changed man.

As for when I'll see you again (and kiss you again, you better believe it!), do you have plans after school? Would you like—ahem—to study together, perhaps? You could come to my apartment, and this time I could be in charge of snacks. I make a mean plate of nachos, and by "mean," I mean without a doubt the cheesiest, saltiest, ooey-gooey-ist nachos you've ever tasted. (And the manliest nachos you've ever had as well. I say this because it occurs to me that "ooey-gooey-ist," while absolutely true, might possibly read as a tad bit, ah, epicene.[1] Have

I been spending too much time in the company of ten-year-old girls?)

We could, while munching on nachos, even get some actual work done.

Possibly.

1. How's them apples, hmm? By which I mean: Are you impressed by my impressive[2] vocabulary?

2. Yikes. "Impressed" and "impressive" in the same sentence—now that is <u>not</u> impressive.[3]

3. I see that I also used "mean" three times in the same sentence, when I was bragging about my nachos. I then used it a 4th time in my first footnote,[4] and a 5th time in this here footnote. Altogether unimpressive!

4. But do I get bonus points[5] for using footnotes in the first place?

5. Better: bonus kisses?[6] Especially for using foot-notes within footnotes . . .

6. Here's hoping.

Enjoy your morning, sweet M. I'll catch you at lunch.

—John

Yaz sighs. She's made it all the way to the end of the back-and-forth without fainting or hyperventilating once. Which is good!

She, on the other hand, is bad. A bad girl. A snoop and a Nosy Nelly and a sneaky little fifth grader whose teachers trusted her, and whose trust she betrayed.

She refolds the note, careful to stay on the pre-creased lines. She pushes herself to her feet, smooths her *hijab,* and brushes off her jeans.

And now go back to class, she tells herself. *Go back to class and give Ms. Perez the note and pretend like nothing has changed.*

She'll have to use her best acting skills, of course, because everything *has* changed, and not just the way she sees her teachers. The way she sees herself has changed, too, and she senses there's no going back.

She had no idea that being bad could feel so ridiculously delicious.

camilla

id you ask your mom if you can go to dinner?" Max says, catching Milla alone by the pencil
sharpener. It wasn't hard, being caught. Milla knows that
the pencil sharpener is one of Max's favorite places, so
Milla went there hoping Max would catch her. Because
she has good news! She did ask her Mom Abigail about
going to the Olive Garden, and Mom Abigail said yes!!!

Only now, with Max less than a foot away from her,
she finds herself unable to make her throat work.

"Milla?" Max says.

She smiles anxiously. She ducks her head, then peers up at him from under her eyelashes.

"Oh, crud," Max says, thonking his head. "Did you ask your *moms*, I mean. Plural. Both of them. I, uh, wasn't suggesting you only have one, because I know you don't. I totally know that you have two moms, which is totally cool."

Milla waves away his words. She's not offended when people say "mom" instead of "moms," unless the person who says it is trying to offend her. And Max isn't, because Max never would. He's not that sort of boy. He's the sort of boy who is adorkable and sweet in his usual uniform of jeans paired with a shirt from his favorite website, Think Geek. Today's shirt says, I AM NOT IGNORING YOU. YOUR COMMENT IS AWAITING MODERATION.

Except Max looks as if he's the one whose comment is awaiting moderation. Which it is, technically. He shifts his weight from one foot to the other, and Milla realizes that by making him wait, she's making *him* feel anxious.

"Yes," she forces herself to say, and once the word is out, *phew*. All the scared feelings *whoosh* out of her.

"Yes, you asked your moms?" Max says. "Or yes, they said yes?"

"Both," Milla says happily. "I asked my Mom Abigail, and she said sure, and that she's looking forward to getting to know your mom better. She says it'll be fun."

"It will be," Max says. "So, would tomorrow night work? The Olive Garden has unlimited breadsticks, you know."

Milla giggles.

"What's so funny?" someone says grouchily, and Milla does a double take. It's Katie-Rose. The real Katie-Rose, suddenly standing *right here beside them* even though she's not even in Mr. Emerson's class.

"Why are *you* here?" Milla asks. *And how much did you hear? When Max and I were talking . . . how much did you overhear???*

"Geez-o-criminy," Katie-Rose says. "Bite my head off, why don't you?"

"I just . . . I didn't . . ." Milla exhales and tries again. "Are you running errands for Ms. Perez now?"

"No."

"Then…?"

"I had to escape," Katie-Rose says. "Somebody in my class was being a jerk. Somebody named Preston." She gives Max a dark look, as if it's Max's fault, whatever Preston did.

Milla steps closer to him. To Katie-Rose, she says, "Well, does Ms. Perez know you're here?"

Katie-Rose shrugs.

"So you're just randomly roaming the building."

"I could be in the bathroom," Katie-Rose says.

"But you're not, and now it's time to go bye-bye," Milla tells her friend, taking Katie-Rose's shoulders and steering her toward the door.

Katie-Rose twists easily out of Milla's grasp.

Milla sighs. She tries a new tactic, pointing toward Violet's desk. "Look, there's Violet. Why don't you go say hi to Violet?"

Katie-Rose scowls. "Violet is busy, that's why."

Milla draws her thumbnail to her mouth. The new girl, Hayley, has scooted her chair over next to Violet's, and they're sharing Violet's desk. Milla's not sure how she feels about their new coziness, actually, but right now she's got other, more pressing concerns on her mind. Anyway, Violet and Hayley aren't doing anything wrong. They're working on their "Where I'm From" poems. Milla should be doing the same, as should Max. It *is* school, after all.

And Katie-Rose should go away.

"Mr. Emerson?" Milla says. "How much longer do we have to work on our poems?"

Katie-Rose makes an indignant sound and stomps on Milla's toe. Milla doesn't even care, almost.

Mr. Emerson lifts his head. "Oh, about ten minutes. How's that sound?"

"Okay, thanks," Milla says. *Look who is next to me*, she adds telepathically. *Look, look, look.*

"Excuse me . . . Katie-Rose?" Mr. Emerson says. "Can I help you?"

Katie-Rose plays dumb. "No, I'm good." She plasters on a fake smile. "Um . . . hi!"

Mr. Emerson gets up from his desk and heads toward them.

"Geez-o-criminy," Katie-Rose mutters. "Thanks a lot, Milla."

"What?" Milla says. "And why do you keep saying that? 'Geez-o-criminy'?"

"Because Sam said it this morning, and it's funny. Because I want to, okay? And for the record, it's copyrighted, and you can't use it, not even with Max." She lifts her eyebrows. "*Especially* with Max."

This makes Milla blush, which is unfair because she is not the one who randomly showed up and butted her way into a perfectly nice pencil-sharpener conversation.

"All right, Katie-Rose, the door's that way," Mr. Emerson says, gesturing at the door. "Off you go."

Katie-Rose storms off without a good-bye. Max blows out a big breath.

"Girls are so confusing," he says, and the *way* he says it—totally bewildered, totally lost—makes Mr. Emerson laugh.

"You got that right, buddy," he says. He winks at Milla, who's glad that Katie-Rose is gone, but who also feels guilty for her role in making it happen. "But sometimes they're pretty cool, too."

fourteen

Violet

Hayley's nice. During lunch, she makes a point of being not just friendly, but extra friendly, and Violet thinks that's really cool, especially since Hayley is the new girl. She *could* just sit quietly and say nothing, and no one would think less of her.

Instead, Hayley chats and smiles and pushes her bag of jalapeño-cheddar potato chips to the center of the table, labeling them "up for grabs" for anyone who wants any. Not only that, but she makes an effort to *connect* with Milla and Yasaman and even Katie-Rose, who's acting even more prickly than normal today.

And since Violet and Hayley have already connected (sort of, anyway), Violet is content to sit back and enjoy.

Hayley compliments Milla on her snazzy reusable lunch bag. "Kinda puts mine to shame, doesn't it?" she says, lifting the corner of the bag her food was in. It's not even a brown-paper lunch sack. It's just a plastic bag from the grocery store, the kind Violet's elderly neighbors use as "pooper scooper" bags for their Schnauzer.

"I wish my uncle would buy me a cute lunch bag," Hayley goes on. "But yeah, right. Like *that's* ever going to happen." She indicates Milla's tote. "Yours is fancy, isn't it? Not just cute, but *fancy* fancy. Expensive fancy. Like the Prada of lunch bags or something."

Milla can't decide whether to be pleased or embarrassed, Violet can tell.

"It's Dooney and Bourke," Violet supplies, surprising herself. She's not big on labels, mostly because her mom hates labels and brand names and the snottiness that so often accompanies them. Milla is the opposite of snotty, though. She has super-nice stuff, but she never brags about it.

"Sweet," Hayley says. She takes a bite of her sandwich, which from the looks of it is bologna on white bread and nothing more. The circle-shaped slice of bologna sticks out beyond the straight line of the bread's pale crust. It reminds Violet of her days in Atlanta, where people actually ate bologna and thought it was just as normal as turkey or ham. Here, in Thousand Oaks, California, Violet doesn't think she's ever seen anyone eat bologna.

"Um, you could tell your uncle it would be good for the environment," Milla says. "If you got an insulated lunch tote, I mean. Because you'd use it every day, and so you wouldn't, you know, be adding plastic to the landfill."

Hayley laughs. "Is that what it's called? An 'insulated lunch tote'?" Milla's cheeks pinken, and Hayley adds, "No, no, that's *awesome*. It's just, no one at Stanton Heights brought their lunches to school in *insulated lunch totes*."

"Oh," Milla says. She blinks, and Violet suspects she knows why. When everyone first sat down, Hayley shared bits and pieces of how she landed here at Rivendell, and Milla is probably still wrapping her head around the fact that Hayley came to Rivendell, which is a private school, from one of Southern California's roughest public schools.

"Anyway, my uncle could give a rat's heiney about the *environment*," Hayley says. Violet isn't sure how to interpret the way Hayley says "environment," drawing it out in a mocking fashion. It could be that Hayley is making fun of her uncle, or it could be that she, Hayley, doesn't give a rat's heiney about the environment, either.

"A rat's heiney," Katie-Rose repeats. She says it in a moody way. "Ha. I'm going to use that expression. I'm going to use that expression on a very specific person who happens to be a very annoying boy. Awesome."

"Does that mean you'll stop saying 'geez-o-criminy'?" Milla asks.

"*No*. Geez-o-criminy. Just because you don't like it doesn't mean I'm not allowed to."

Hayley grins. "'Geez-o-criminy.' *I* like it. It'll drive my uncle nuts."

Milla lifts a spoonful of yogurt to her mouth as if she's at a tea party. Her tone, when she speaks, is bland.

"Hayley, you have to ask Katie-Rose's permission to use 'geez-o-criminy,' because apparently, *geez-o-criminy* is under copyright protection."

Katie-Rose shoots Milla a hurt look. Violet, too, is confused. First Milla got Katie-Rose kicked out of Mr. Emerson's class, and now she's rubbing salt into the wound by bringing up the very thing that led to Katie-Rose getting kicked out?

"It's copyrighted?" Hayley says.

Irritation flashes across Milla's face, only to be immediatly erased. "According to Katie-Rose, yes. According to Katie-Rose, she is the only person allowed to say it, which means that you, Hayley, would be penalized for copyright infringement."

"Omigod, you're so full of it," Hayley says to Milla.

Milla ducks her head. Violet can't be sure, but she seems ashamed.

Hayley turns to Katie-Rose. "That's funny, copyright protection. But she's kidding, right? You don't honestly think you can copyright an expression?"

"I . . . ," Katie-Rose says. "I . . ."

"Omigod, you do!" Hayley crows, and she leans across the table and holds up her hand to give Katie-Rose a high five. Katie-Rose wrinkles her forehead, but tentatively touches her palm to Hayley's.

"Dude, you're hysterical," Hayley says to her. "*Copyright infringement*, omigod. You know what you should copyright is *that*, the right to copyright your expressions! You could make a killing!"

Katie-Rose's smile, which was wobbly for a second, firms up. "Well, first of all, I *am* hysterical. I agree." She makes a face at Milla, who pretends she can't be bothered by it. "And second of all, if I'm the one who comes up with a particular expression, then I *should* get to say who can use it or not. So thank you, Hayley, and I applaud your good taste. And as a reward, *yes*, you can use 'geez-o-criminy.'"

Hayley dips her head. "Why, thank you."

Milla clears her throat.

"Yes?" Katie-Rose says.

"Just to clarify . . . and Katie-Rose, thank you so much for sharing all this excellent knowledge . . . but 'geez-o-criminy' *is* an expression *you* came up with, right?" Milla asks.

Katie-Rose narrows her eyes. "That's private information. Classified. And speaking of classified information, *Milla*, is this really the time to spill people's secrets? Do we—and by *we*, I mean *you*—really want to go there?"

"I do," Hayley says. She scans the faces of the flower friends. "I love secrets. Katie-Rose, do you have a secret?"

Katie-Rose playacts a scarily innocent smile. "No, no secrets for me."

"Milla?" Hayley says, focusing on the next most likely candidate.

Milla is bright red. "No."

"*Everyone* has secrets," Yasaman says, and Violet realizes that this is the first remark Yaz has made during all of lunch.

"Well, let's hear them!" Hayley exclaims.

Violet doesn't know what Yaz is referring to. What does she mean, "everyone has secrets"? Does *Yaz* have a secret?

For a moment, possibilities seem to flicker over Yaz's

expression. For a moment, it seems as if Yaz has something to share. Then the moment passes, and she says, "If we told our secrets, they wouldn't be secrets anymore."

Hayley's shoulders slump. "Oh, poo. But fine. What should we talk about instead, then?"

The flower friends are silent. Violet wonders if the lunch is going as well as she thought it was after all. To fix things, she picks the most harmless topic she can think of, harmless and yet fun.

"Candy," she says. "Everyone go around and say your favorite candy bar."

"Candy!" Katie-Rose says, brightening up. "I love candy. What if my favorite kind of candy isn't a candy bar, though?"

"That's fine," Violet says, and off Katie-Rose goes, launching into a monologue comparing Junior Mints to Mike and Ike Hot Tamales.

"What about green apple sour loops?" Yaz says. "I thought they were your favorite."

"Only on Saturdays," Katie-Rose proclaims, making everyone laugh.

"What?" Katie-Rose says. "On Saturdays, my taste

buds are different. Is that a hard concept to under-stand?"

"Um, yes," Milla says.

Violet's chest loosens.

She pops another one of Hayley's chips into her mouth. It's spicy and makes her eyes water.

Later, like almost seven hours later, she IMs Katie-Rose. She wants to make sure that what she was feeling was what Katie-Rose was feeling, too. Because Katie-Rose, when it comes to new friends . . . well, Violet knows that Katie-Rose will be the hardest nut to crack in terms of getting her to let someone new into their circle.

But certain conversations are easier to have in written words instead of spoken words, so she fires up her computer and starts typing:

Chat with The*rose*Knows	
Ultraviolet:	Katie-Rose! hi hi!
The*rose*Knows:	well, hellllllooooooooo, Violet-o.
	wassup?
Ultraviolet:	nothing. Just saying hi. hi!

The*rose*Knows: +looks at Violet strangely+

Ultraviolet: fine. I just wanted . . .

Ultraviolet: I just wanted . . .

The*rose*Knows: r u stuttering? While instnant messaging???

Ultraviolet: "instnant"? at least I know how to spell!

Ultraviolet: anyway, u shldn't make fun of stuttering.

The*rose*Knows: who says I was?

Ultraviolet: ok, whateves. Weirdo. I just wanted to talk about lunch today. You know.

The*rose*Knows: um, yes, I know we had lunch today. Yr point?

Ultraviolet: ur acting dumb on purpose!

Ultraviolet: I'm talking about HAYLEY. What did you think of Hayley?!!!

The*rose*Knows: +shrugs+

The*rose*Knows: she was nice

Ultraviolet: she was?

Ultraviolet: yeah, she was, wasn't she?!!!! 😊

The*rose*Knows: u act surprised. R u surprised?

Ultraviolet: NO!

Ultraviolet: I'm not. It's just . . .

Ultraviolet: So lunch was good, right? Everyone was good? Everyone had fun?

The*rose*Knows: I'm sorry, who's the weirdo?

The*rose*Knows: ur acting obsessed

Ultraviolet: sorry. ur right. sorry!

Ultraviolet: but I'm just glad, that's all.

Ultraviolet: and . . . thx, k-r

The*rose*Knows: for what?

Ultraviolet: um, for being u?

The*rose*Knows: hmmph. Ur very welcome. +bows+

The*rose*Knows: and now good night, weirdo!!!!!

Thursday, November 17

Yasaman struggles to stay focused on her schoolwork all morning long. All she can think about when she looks at her teacher is the . . . what-it-is that's going on between her and Mr. Emerson. It is adorable, but also unnerving! She wants her teachers to be happy (especially Ms. Perez), and she thinks it would be great if they got married and had kids and—ooo!—named their baby girl Yasaman. They should, after all, given the role Yaz has played in their romance.

But then, on the other hand, the romance aspect of it all freaks her out. It is so real, and grown-up-ish, and involves actual love letters that Yasaman has actually read. She is not sure she is ready to know about a grown-up romance. She might even be sure she's not. Except that it's exciting, and anyway, it's too late, because she already does know and there's no going back.

It makes it difficult to concentrate on her vocabulary quiz. And her multiplication facts and everything.

Hottie-with-a-body, she thinks. *Magical evenings. Bonus kisses.* Aaagh! Yaz doesn't know how to put away all of this thrilling-slash-disturbing knowledge she accidentally learned. Except she didn't "accidentally" learn it at all, did she?

She doesn't know what to do with that piece of the puzzle, either.

She wasn't lying yesterday when she said that everyone in the whole wide world has secrets. Just, some secrets are too big to hold in, and Yaz is fairly sure she'll explode if she has to keep the contents of Ms. Perez and Mr. Emerson's note to herself for much longer. She wanted to tell her flower friends about the notes, but she felt like she shouldn't. Like it would be a betrayal of her teachers' privacy. But maybe Ms. Perez and Mr. Emerson shouldn't have been passing notes during school, anyway. Did they think of that? And maybe they shouldn't have asked Yasaman to be their delivery girl, either. Did they think of that???

The bottom line is that yes, Yaz is happy that Mr. Emerson and Ms. Perez—or John and Maria—are, ah, getting along so well. But knowing about their study dates and their nachos, and especially about their kissing (!!!), is *waaaaaay* more stressful than Yaz could have imagined, so when Ms. Perez releases the class for morning break, Yaz is up and out of her desk like a bullet.

Yaz worms past Natalia and Chance and Preston, and she reaches the door that leads to the playground before any of them.

"Yaz?" she hears through the muzzy-buzzing of her thoughts. It's Katie-Rose. She's probably wondering why her friend has suddenly turned into an Olympic-class sprinter. "Yaz?!"

Yaz could stop running and let Katie-Rose catch up with her and spill everything to Katie-Rose right now, even though Katie-Rose would gag and make vomit noises and be totally horrified that two teachers are acting so lovey-dovey. But the cold air is a tonic to Yasaman's flushed skin. Her muscles burn as she sprints down the field, and it feels good. Her lungs are tight, and her heart thumps against her ribcage, and oh, that's good, too, because it leaves nothing left for thinking.

"Yasaman!" she hears.

She runs.

"Yasaman!"

Her shirt pulls against her chest. Someone's grabbed it, trying to make her stop. She keeps going, pulling against the tugging, but she can't run forever. Anyway, she's ready to talk now. She thinks. Once she catches her breath, that is.

She leans over, sucking wind and bearing her weight on her thighs.

"Yaz?"

Yasaman turns, panting.

"Violet," she says between gasps. She was expecting Katie-Rose.

Violet's forehead is lined with worry. Unlike Yaz, who is huffing and puffing, Violet is elegant and perfectly unmussed.

"Are you okay?" Violet says. "What's going on? Is something wrong?"

Yaz shakes her head. Then she nods her head. She holds up one finger to say *give me a second*, and takes in great gulps of the cool November air. Then she straightens her spine and drags the back of her hand across her sweaty forehead.

Violet regards her. "Let's walk," she says, linking her arm through Yasaman's.

"Good idea," Yaz says.

They start off along "the loop," as Rivendell calls it. It's the broadest circle you can make within the confines of the playground, right alongside the metal fence that separates the playground from Lemay Avenue at one end and the somewhat spooky railroad tracks at the other.

Yasaman's breathing grows more regular. Violet strolls patiently, not pressing. She doesn't unhook her arm from Yasaman's.

"So," Yaz says at last.

"So," Violet repeats.

Yaz gives a sideways peek at her friend. "I needed to run."

"I gathered."

"My brain was spinning."

"I've felt that way before," Violet says. They take several more steps. "How come? If you want to tell me, that is."

"I do," Yaz says. She means it, too. She checks to make sure no one is nearby, then stops walking and confesses everything, all in a rush: Mr. Emerson. Ms. Perez. Dating and kissing and sending each other sweet (but somewhat disturbing!) love notes, and all of this right under Yasaman's nose!!!

Violet's eyes grow wider and wider with each new detail. When Yaz finally stops talking, she closes her eyes and keeps them closed for a long moment. Then she opens them with a snap. "*Wow*," she says.

"Exactly."

Violet starts walking again. Yaz matches her pace.

"They shouldn't have used you as a messenger," she says.

"I know," Yaz says.

"But . . . it's kind of cool that they did."

"I know."

"It's kind of exciting, even."

Yaz sighs. "I *know*."

"So the question is, did anything bad happen? Do you feel like you need to tell Ms. Westerfeld or anything?"

Ms. Westerfeld? The *principal*? "No!" Yaz exclaims. "Omigoodness, Violet. If I told Ms. Westerfeld . . ." She shudders, imagining her teachers getting in trouble. Surely they would . . . wouldn't they? "Why would I tell Ms. Westerfeld?"

"Well, apparently you wouldn't," Violet says. "So we answered that question. So, good."

Yes, good. Yaz nods, relieved.

"And we always have said how cute they'd be together," Violet goes on. She squeezes Yaz's elbow. "You, especially, thought they'd be cute together."

Yaz nods again.

"And now they really are together, so that's another good thing. But I do think you should demand to be their flower girl when they get married."

Yaz giggles. It feels as if a too-tight shoelace around her insides has finally been loosened. "I was thinking they should name their firstborn child after me."

"Absolutely," Violet argues. "Unless it's a boy, in which case maybe they'll name him after Mr. Emerson."

"John Junior," Yaz says.

"Well…unless they use his nickname. Mr. E's, I mean."

"Huh?"

"C'mon. Can't you just see it?" Violet pretends to be Ms. Perez, holding a little baby. "And here is our little darling, Hottie-with-a-Body. We call him Hottie for short."

"Agh!" Yaz cries, covering both of her ears with her hands. She giggles and giggles and *giggles*.

Violet grins. She waits until Yaz has calmed down, and says, "But hey, I don't think you should worry about…you know. Reading their notes or whatever."

"You don't? You don't think it was wrong of me?"

"Well, sure it was wrong. But in the big picture, I don't think you need to worry about it."

"Explain."

"You said you're not going to tell on them. You said you don't want to tell on them. So that means your conscience doesn't think you need to tell on them, and so *that* means"—Violet shrugs—"that even your conscience isn't freaking out about it. You might be, but not your conscience, and Yaz? You have a very strong conscience."

"I do?"

"You do."

"I do," Yaz says. She lets the truth flood in. With it comes a tidal wave of relief.

"So I don't need to *do* anything? Like, for example, tell Ms. Perez I read her personal and private love notes?"

"Why in the world would you do that?" Violet says. She stops walking and stares across the field. She puts her hand over her eyes and squints.

"But what if they ask me to pass more notes?"

"If you don't want to, just tell them no," Violet says. She changes course, veering across the field instead of continuing along the loop. "Unless you don't mind, that is."

"I don't know if I do or not. Would you, if you were me?"

Violet seems distracted. "Huh?"

"If Mr. Emerson asked you to take a note to Ms. Perez, would you?"

"Yaz, hold that thought. Um, we'll talk later, all right?"

"Why later?" She grabs Violet's arm. "We're talking now, so why can't we keep talking now?"

"I just . . ." Violet shoots her a tight smile. "I can't."

Yaz knits her brow. "Why? What's wrong?"

"Nothing, I hope. But I've got to run, 'kay?"

She pulls free, and Yaz watches, perplexed and more than a little dismayed, as Violet hurries over to the play structure.

Oh, Yaz thinks, putting the pieces together. It's Hayley. Violet's worried about Hayley because Hayley's standing by the slide, surrounded by Modessa, Quin, and Elena. They're standing awfully close. Menacingly close. The four of them are talking, but Yaz can't make out what they're saying.

Violet reaches them, and Yaz's breath hitches. Two minutes ago, Violet's elbow was hooked through Yasaman's. Now she's elbowing her way into Modessa's little circle, and Yaz doesn't like it one bit. She doesn't want Hayley to get hurt, but she doesn't want Violet to get hurt, either.

If anyone's going to get hurt. In all honesty, she doesn't know what to think of the scene unfolding before her. She knows that Modessa and her buddies are bad news, but she doesn't know if Hayley agrees. She doesn't know if the Evil Chicks are even being mean to Hayley, or to Violet. She's too far away to tell.

She knows what she *feels*, though. Violet was helping *her*, and then she decided to run off and help Hayley instead.

It doesn't feel good.

Sixteen

Violet

"Oh my God," Modessa says in the way that only Modessa can. Like, if Violet were writing it out in poem form, with line breaks and other clues to the reader, it would look like this:

OH

(beat)

(beat)

my**GOD**.

But that's Modessa, dripping with attitude.

Violet steps closer. So far, the group hasn't noticed her.

"And these were your friends?" Modessa says to Hayley.

"I know," Hayley says.

"Some friends!" Modessa says.

"I know," Hayley says. She looks over Modessa's shoulder. "Hi, Violet."

Modessa twirls on her heel. Violet's insides sink, and then she squeezes her hands into fists.

You are strong, she reminds herself. *So be strong.*

"Hi," she says stiffly.

"Violet," Modessa says, the way another person might say, *Gross, a dead roach.* "Why are you here?"

"Why are *you* here?" Violet replies.

It's not the most brilliant response, and Modessa takes full advantage. "Um, because I am? But *you*. You're such a *magnet*. Everywhere I go, there you are. It's annoying and pathetic. Am I right, girls?"

Quin and Elena nod. Their heads are attached to invisible strings, because they're Modessa's puppets.

"Hayley—" Violet says.

"*No*," Modessa interrupts. "Don't try to steal Hayley away, and don't follow her around, either. Don't follow any of us. Anyway, can't you tell that poor Hayley doesn't want you bugging her?"

Poor Hayley? Violet thinks. *Poor Hayley?!*

Modessa very deliberately turns her back on Violet. *Done*, her actions say. And *bye-bye to you*. To Hayley, she says, "Well, real friends wouldn't have done that."

Done what? Violet wonders. She does feel dumb, standing outside their circle. Should she leave?

But no. Because Modessa is clearly making her bid for Hayley. Violet can't back down.

"Come to my house, and I'll do it," Modessa says.

Violet edges closer. *Do what?*

Hayley makes a noise that's neither a *yes* nor a *no*. "I don't know. I'm, like, not sure anymore. That I even want to."

Want to do what?! Violet's mind demands.

"I think you should," Modessa proclaims. "I totally think you should, and I totally think you should let me be the one to do it for you." She moves closer to Hayley, farther from Violet. Quin and Elena follow suit. "Okay? So will you?"

They're cornering her, Violet thinks. Then she doubts herself, because Hayley does have legs, after all. And, unlike Elena, she has a functioning spine. Hayley could walk away from Modessa if she wanted to, because unlike Quin and Elena, Hayley isn't a puppet-girl.

But if Hayley isn't a puppet-girl, then why is she putting up with the Evil Chicks? And what does Hayley maybe or maybe not want to do, and how does it involve Modessa?

Violet forces herself to step forward. "Modessa?" Her voice quivers, dang it. "Leave Hayley alone."

Modessa rolls her eyes at Quin, Elena, and Hayley . . . *and all of them giggle.*

Even Hayley.

Violet swallows. She's suddenly uncertain whose side Hayley is on.

"What's your problem, Violet?" Modessa says, as if even such a simple exchange is exhausting.

"Yes, what's your problem, *magnet*?" Quin contributes, sniggering.

Violet glares, shifting her focus to Modessa's right-hand girl. She pulls herself up and ignores the niggling awareness that by taking on Quin, she's taking the easy way out. "Shut up, Quin. Anyway, you need to pay more attention during science, because a *magnet* draws things toward it. So who's the magnet?"

Quin looks confused. Elena looks confused. Then Elena's brow unwrinkles, and she says, "*Ohhhh.*" She turns to Modessa. "She's right."

"Huh?" Quin says.

"Modessa's the magnet," Elena says.

This gives Violet the courage to glance at Hayley.

Hayley's expression is impassive.

"She's not right, and shut up," Modessa snaps. She pauses. "No, she *is* right, actually, but not in the way she thinks. I am a magnet, because I have a magnetic personality, just like movie stars and America's Next Top Models." She lifts her chin. "So thank you, Violet, for clearing that up."

Modessa smiles at her. It's not a real smile.

"Violet's a very smart girl," Modessa says. "Don't you think, Hayley? That Violet's a very smart girl?"

Violet turns to Hayley, hoping that she will somehow fix things.

"Whatever you say," Hayley replies.

It's an answer, but it only leaves Violet with more questions.

Seventeen

Katie-Rose

On Thursday afternoons, Katie-Rose and Yasaman take trapeze lessons in Rivendell's PE room, which has been set up with basic trapeze equipment just for that purpose. It's pretty much awesome sauce in a can . . . or rather, awesome sauce flying through the air with the greatest of ease! Only without splattering onto the floor, hopefully, because a) that would be gross, like vomit, and b) it could result in bodily harm.

No one splatters today. Yaz even pulls off a tricky level-three skill involving a reverse single knee hang followed by a double somersault over the bar. The hardest part about a double somersault, or a single somersault for that matter, is when it comes time to let go of the bar and land, not on your booty but on your feet. It's hard because your brain gets confused when it does loop-de-loops, that's Katie-Rose's theory. Brains expect to be perched on top of necks, and they expect, in general, to stay up there and not go bouncing all around town.

But add in a somersault . . .

Suffice it to say that unlike Yaz, Katie-Rose has yet to master the single somersault dismount or the double somersault dismount. Oh well. Katie-Rose doesn't care. She likes swinging on the bar best of all, anyway.

After the class ends, Katie-Rose jogs to catch Yasaman before she exits the building.

"Yaz, hold up!" she calls. "Where's the fire?"

Yaz turns around. "Huh?" She looks from side to side. "Fire? Where?"

Katie-Rose says, "Oh, Yaz," because she's so funny, that silly girl. "There's no fire, you goof. I just mean, why are you rushing out of here so fast?"

Yasaman tilts her head. She's wearing her "sports" *hijab*, which is one solid color and made out of stretchy material. The *hijabs* Yaz wears during the day are long and flowing and made from beautiful, intricately woven fabric, and compared to them, her sports *hijab* is startlingly boring.

"I'm sure my mom's waiting for me, that's all," Yaz says. "She doesn't like me to keep her waiting."

Well, yes, Katie-Rose does know that. Yaz's parents are stricter than Katie-Rose's. Stricter than the parents of any of the FFF's. Still, Katie-Rose doesn't want Yaz to go just yet.

"Nice double somersault dismount," Katie-Rose says.

Yaz's face brightens, and the before-and-after difference between Yaz's two expressions makes Katie-Rose realize that Yaz wasn't looking very sunshiny until now.

"Thanks," Yaz says. "You did a good job, too, on your cutaway."

Katie-Rose waves that off. "Level-one skill. A baby could do it."

"Hardly. A baby would fall off."

"My point exactly. *I* fell off."

"But you got back on. You have to remember that. You can't just focus on the bad stuff."

Bad stuff. Huh. The phrase strikes a chord with Katie-Rose, and she uses it as an opening to get to what she really wants to discuss.

"Okay, true," Katie-Rose says. "But speaking of bad stuff, do you feel like things are weird between us, Yaz? Not you and me, but all of us? Milla and Violet and you and me?"

"N-n-no," Yaz says, but doubt flickers across her face.

"Because it was you who said that whole thing about secrets, at lunch yesterday. Are you telling me you don't feel like everyone's keeping . . . well . . . secrets from each other?"

A stronger emotion shadows Yasaman's face. Yaz ducks her head and tries to pass Katie-Rose, but Katie-Rose grabs her. She stares deep into Yaz's eyes. "Yaz?"

Yaz looks away.

"*Yaz?*" Katie-Rose steps to the side until she's once again within Yaz's line of vision. "Talk to me."

"Did Violet tell you?" Yaz asks.

"Did Violet tell me what?"

Yaz is flustered.

"Did Violet tell me *what*?" Katie-Rose repeats.

"Okay, listen," Yaz says. "Maybe I do have a secret. Do *you*?"

"Maybe I do, maybe I don't," Katie-Rose says.

Yaz deflates. That's what it looks like.

"Yes!" Katie-Rose says. "I do, I do. Will you tell me yours if I tell you mine?"

Yaz glances toward the main door of the building. "My mom's waiting. I've got to go."

"Milla has a date with Max tonight," Katie-Rose says quickly. "A *date* date. Like, you know, smoochie-smoochie, and you know how I feel about all that."

"I do?"

"Yes, that it's gross," Katie-Rose says. She sounds too forceful, even to herself, and for the barest flash of an instant, Katie-Rose glimpses her *true* secret, which is that she's jealous of Milla and Max. Because until yesterday, when Preston made everyone laugh at her, she honestly thought he liked her. But no. Only Milla gets to have a boy like her. Not Katie-Rose.

Well, that line of thought isn't going to get her any-where. "They're going to the Olive Garden, and I'm going to go, too," she announces. "Only Milla doesn't know."

Yasaman's face changes. "Wait. First of all, I thought Milla wasn't . . ." She shakes her head. "Never mind. What do you mean, you're going to go, too?"

"Exactly that: I'm going to go, too. She's not the only one allowed to go to the Olive Garden, is she?"

Yaz looks confused. "But . . . are you going because you want to? Or because Milla is?"

Huh? What kind of a question is that? Katie-Rose asks herself.

The kind you don't want to answer, another part of her answers.

She pushes the issue aside and breezes on. "As soon as I get home, I'm going to beg and whine for toys, only instead of toys, I'll say, 'Please-oh-please can't we go out for dinner at the Olive Garden? And have family time? Because family time is very-super-a-lot important to a young girl's development of healthiness and self-esteem?' And I'll quote their slogan, which that chef dude says on TV: 'When you're here, you're family.'"

Yasaman stares at her. "You're nuts."

"Well. Maybe." Frankly, Katie-Rose thought Yasaman would be more interested in Milla's date. "Anyway, that's my secret. What's yours?"

"I don't think Milla's going to be happy if you randomly show up at her date," Yaz says slowly.

Katie-Rose groans. This is what Yasaman is going to focus on? This one small detail? "I'm not going to plop down in her lap, Yaz. Geez-o-criminy." Her lips twitch. "That would be kind of awesome, though. Or if I plopped down in Max's lap? Ha! 'Hi, peeps! It's me, Katie-Rose-o the fabuloso!'"

"I don't think you should," Yasaman repeats. "Plus, in terms of friend weirdness, that's only going to make it worse."

Katie-Rose hears something in Yasaman's tone. "So you *do* think we're having friend weirdnesses."

"I didn't say that," Yaz says.

"But you didn't deny it. Listen, Yaz. I told you my secret, so you better tell me yours. *Now.*"

"I said I *maybe* had a secret, but I don't. Honest."

"Does it have to do with me?" Katie-Rose says.

Yaz gives her a look.

"Does it have to do with Milla? Does it have to do with Violet?"

"No," Yaz says. "Stop asking, because it's nothing. I mean, there is nothing. No secret."

"There is, and it has to do with Violet," Katie-Rose says, watching Yasaman's face closely. She thinks back over Violet's behavior this week. Her eyebrows go up. "Does it have to do with Hayley?"

"No!" Yaz says. "*Shhh!*"

"Are you *jealous* of Hayley? Is that your secret?"

Yasaman presses her lips together.

"It is!" Katie-Rose exclaims. "Omigosh!"

"I'm not jealous," Yaz says. "I do, however, have to go. I'll, um, talk to you later." She strides toward the glass doors that lead to Rivendell's parking lot, and sure enough, her mom's car is the very first car in the pickup lane.

Yaz leaves the building. Katie-Rose follows on Yaz's heels and waves at Yaz's mom.

"One sec, Mrs. Tercan!" Katie-Rose calls. "I need to ask Yasaman a question about homework."

Mrs. Tercan checks her watch. "It is late, *habibti*,"

she tells Yasaman. "We need to make dinner for your *baba*."

Katie-Rose holds up her finger and makes puppy-dog eyes. "One second? Please?" To Yaz, she says, "You were the one who first wanted to be nice to Hayley, remember?"

"I still do."

"Do you?"

"I'm not jealous of Hayley," Yaz insists.

Katie-Rose studies her. She takes in her pink cheeks, her downcast eyes, the way she clasps her hands behind her back. Katie-Rose takes all of this in, and although she was ready to gloat, she has a change of heart. It's no fun to feel jealous of someone.

"Okay," Katie-Rose says. "I believe you."

Beep-beep. It's Mrs. Tercan. "Yasaman, come along," she says.

"I've got to go," Yaz says. "Bye."

Katie-Rose watches Yaz climb into her mom's van. As soon as they drive off, doubt kicks in. Yaz, jealous? Of Hayley? It felt right for a moment . . . but surely not.

She might have stood there longer, wondering about Yaz and Hayley and who knows what else, but she's pulled out of her reverie by the distinctive honk of her mom's Volvo station wagon. It's more of a *henk* than a honk, maybe because Volvos are Swedish.

"Hey, kiddo," Katie-Rose's mom calls. The driver-side window whirs down as she speaks. "We've got to get going. It's five thirty, and I have yet to figure out anything for dinner."

Dinner! *Dinner.* Right.

"Don't you worry, Mom-babe," Katie-Rose says. She walks around her mom's car and climbs in on the passenger's side. "I've got dinner all figured out."

"Oh, do you?" her mom says, amused.

"I do, because yes, I *am* that awesome."

Eighteen

Camilla

eing at the Olive Garden with Max is more stressful than Milla thought it could be, and that's saying *a lot.*

Sitting next to Max? With her mom and Max's mom across from them, so that they form a kid/mom square with bread sticks in the middle? The moms were supposed to sit at their own table. But surprise! The hostess brought them all to this one single table, and no one argued against it.

Milla doubts it makes much of a difference. With or without the moms, she would be freaking. Her breaths are so shallow and rapid that she truly might:

A) faint

B) see stars and be struck with a sudden case of restaurant blindness, resulting in a nosedive onto the table or a backward chair-fall onto the hard tile floor

C) choke on the wad of breadstick that will not go down and will not go down, because she's too busy fast-breathing to get much chewing done

D) all of the above

These are legitimate worries. In fact, she's beginning to see stars already. Her vision is tunneling in on her, and she turns to tell Max that this was all a big mistake and she's going to have to go now, sorry. But she can't speak, she discovers. All she can do is focus on Max's face, and thank goodness it's a cute face, or think how much worse it would be!

Uh-oh. It's moving, the face. *Max's* face. He's leaning closer, and his mouth is making word shapes, but what do the word shapes sound like?

You know this boy! Milla tells herself. *Get it together! THIS IS MAX, AND YOU CAN DO THIS!*

"…right?" Max says.

Milla's chest balloons outward with relief. The buzzing in her head has subsided, and her hearing is back—hooray!

"Right!" she echoes.

Mom Abigail and Max's mom laugh. Milla does, too, though she's confused.

Max cocks his head. "Huh?"

Uh-oh. The head buzzing's coming back. *Fight it, fight it!* Milla tells herself.

"I'm sorry, what?" she says, super polite. Then—oh, dreadful—she has to lift her napkin to her mouth and spit out the wad of breadstick. It is glue. It is sticky. It has to go.

"The poem we're supposed to finish tomorrow," Max says. He peers at her, but he is a friendly peer-er. A smile tugs at his lips, like he thinks she's cute even if she's making no sense. "I asked what you decided to write . . . ?"

"Write," she repeats. *Klunk* goes her brain as the pieces fall together. "Write. Right!" The moms laugh again, and Max full-out smiles, and Milla giggles. "*Riiiiight.* Okay. Yeah." She gives an enthusiastic thumbs-up that she immediately wishes she could take back. For one, enthusiastic thumbs-ups are dorky. For two, Milla couldn't care less about the poem assignment, to tell the truth. She likes math better. And drawing.

"Ha ha, yes, um . . ." She sits on her hands. "I haven't really written the whole thing? But it's about my turtle, Tally. Or it will be. I think."

"Your bobble-head turtle?" Max says, and Milla appreciates his respectful tone. He is not the sort of boy who makes fun of a girl's bobble-head turtle. He is *Max*. That is why she is here with him tonight.

"Yeah," she says. "Because Tally helps me. She's my good-luck charm, so that counts as 'Where I'm From.' I mean, I hope it does."

"I think it does," Max says. "That's cool."

Milla's chest loosens even more. It is cool, and just thinking about Tally—that cutie little bobble-head turtle, just the right size to sit in the palm of her hand—has the magical effect of bringing her peace. Milla isn't one hundred percent cured of her nervousness. That would be impossible! But . . . *wow*. She sits up straighter. She takes a sip of water, and it goes down. She doesn't dribble.

"What about you?" she asks Max. "Do you know what you're going to write about?"

"Computers," Max answers promptly. "Programming, coding. HTML. I might do it as a series of haikus. Do you think Mr. Emerson would care?"

"I think he'd love it," Milla says. "He's always wanting us to be creative and stuff."

Mom Abigail chuckles. "*Creative and stuff*," she says to Max's mom, as if illustrating the point that kids say the darnedest things. As if Milla and Max aren't sitting right there across from them, with their ears turned on and everything.

Milla rolls her eyes at Max, who grins.

"But do you think a slash mark counts as a syllable?" Max says.

"What do you mean?"

Max catches his lower lip between his teeth—so adorkable!!!—and he scans the table for those silly crayons the waitress gave them. As if the waitress thought they were five years old instead of ten.

He finds one and scribbles words and symbols on the

back of the goofy kids menu. "Like this. Here's one of my haikus, all right?"

He passes it to Milla:

```
</h1><h2>
This is a poem written
in HTML!
```

"Do you like it?" Max asks.

Milla giggles. It is turning into a night of giggling—which is good! "I don't know what it means," she says.

"Well . . . it means it's written in code," Max says. The tips of his ears turn red. "But, okay, how would you read the first line? If you were reading it out loud."

Milla looks at him from under her eyelashes. His ears turn redder, and Milla feels an odd—but not unpleasant—fluttering in her tummy.

"Um . . . funny-shaped sideways 'V' thing—"

"That's called a caret," Max interrupts.

"A carrot?"

"Technically it's a 'less than' sign, and the other one,

which is called a 'close caret,' is a 'greater than' sign. But I call them carets."

"That's so cute," Milla says.

"It is?" Max's face turns red to match his ears.

"Totally." She slides his poem closer. "Let me try again." She clears her throat. He grins. She reads out loud: "Carrot, slash-mark thing, h—"

"But you don't *say* caret," Max breaks in.

"I don't?"

"No. The caret and the close caret, you don't say either of them, because they're not part of the code. Um, they say, 'The stuff *inside* here is code.'"

"Inside the carrots."

"Inside the carets." Max pushes his hand through his hair. "And. Um. It's just a slash."

"The slash-mark thing?"

"Right."

"Do I say it?"

"Well, yes. But not 'slash-mark thing.' Just 'slash.'"

"Because it's a haiku," Milla says. "So the number of syllables matters."

Max looks relieved. He's so adorable in his relief that

Milla wants to tease him more—to say "the letter h" instead of simply "h," for example—but she cuts him a break. Max and Milla's moms are facing each other, having their own grown-up conversation, but she can tell they're keeping tabs on Milla and Max, too, and Milla doesn't want Max's mother thinking she's dumb.

She clears her throat. She ignores the carrot and makes a mental note to ignore the other carrots—closed and open—that she sees farther on in the first line. "Slash h one h two," she reads. Yep, five syllables, just as it should be. "This is a poem written"—she pauses for the line break—"in HTML!" She puts the menu down. "Awesome! Perfect!"

Max is pleased. "Yeah?"

"Five, seven, five. I love it. I don't get it, but I love it." She takes a bite from her breadstick and has no problem chewing. "What does 'HTML' mean? I've heard of HTML, but I don't know what it stands for."

"High-tech mumbo-lumbo," Max's mom says. Then, covering her mouth, "Oops."

"*Mom-m-m*," Max says.

"Busted," Milla's Mom Abigail says.

Milla lifts her eyebrows at Max. They both knew their moms were eavesdropping, even if everybody was pretending they weren't.

Max gives her a lopsided smile. Then something catches his attention, something two or maybe three feet behind her. His eyes widen, and Milla turns to see.

First, she's confused. Next, she's annoyed. Very annoyed, and perhaps more so than she should be.

But really?

Really?!

"Katie-Rose," Max says.

"Yip!" Katie-Rose chirps. She is perky in her colorful peasant top, her dark hair in its customary high pigtails. "Ha ha. I mean, *yup*! Hello, fellow humans!"

She raises her hand in greeting, and Milla thinks of a Native American maiden welcoming strangers from a strange land. Only they are at the Olive Garden. The Olive Garden is not a far-off land; Max and Milla aren't strangers; and Katie-Rose is the one who doesn't belong. Katie-Rose is not the native here.

Katie-Rose is the *very* unwelcome visitor.

Did she overhear Milla and Max yesterday morning,

when they were talking about the Olive Garden at the pencil sharpener? She must have, and now here she is, trying to mess up Milla's date on purpose.

Beneath the table, Milla squeezes her napkin in her fist. "What are you doing here?" she asks Katie-Rose.

"Studying the migratory patterns of the Canada goose?" Katie-Rose says. No one laughs. "*Eating*, you goof! Or rather, you *goose!*"

No one laughs some more, especially not Milla. Katie-Rose's expression loses its animation.

"It *is* a restaurant," she says. Her voice is smaller than when she first said hello, and shrinks more and more as she speaks. "That's what people do at restaurants. Eat."

So go eat, Milla wants to say. She glares at Katie-Rose. Katie-Rose blinks.

Charlie, Katie-Rose's older brother, marches over and grabs Katie-Rose's arm. "Geez-o-criminy, Katie-Rose. Come on."

She tries to shrug free of him but fails.

"Hi, Milla," Charlie says. He nods at Max, whom he knows because they're neighbors. "Max." He yanks Katie-Rose roughly, and Milla doesn't even care. "It's time to order, and Mom and Dad are pissed you've been gone so long."

Because she's been searching for us, Milla thinks. The Olive Garden is a labyrinth of main rooms, side rooms, and back rooms, and apparently Katie-Rose's family ended up at a table far, far away from Milla and Max's table.

"Bye," Milla says.

"W-w-wait!" Katie-Rose says, stumbling backward as Charlie drags her away. "All I wanted was to say hey!"

"And you did," Milla says. She turns to Max. She shrugs. "She did."

"Yip," Max agrees.

Milla doesn't laugh right away, but when she does, she can't stop. Her anger at Katie-Rose is turned into something much better by Max, and she can't stop laughing even when Max groans and says, "You've got to be kidding me."

"What?" Milla says.

"Preston?" Max says.

Milla looks, and omigosh, it's true. Yet another Rivendell fifth grader has picked tonight of all nights to dine at the Olive Garden, but unlike Katie-Rose, Preston doesn't notice Max and Milla as he and his family walk past them. He's too busy looking over his shoulder, twisting his neck as he tries to catch sight of . . . who? *Katie-Rose?*

Did Preston spot Katie-Rose being dragged backward by her brother as he trailed his family to their table?

So bizarre. But Max zips his lips, and Milla fights successfully to hold in her laughter until Preston is out of range.

"Omigosh," she whispers. Her breath chuffs out of her.

Max shakes his head, his eyes dancing, and Milla is charmed. She no longer cares that Katie-Rose is in the same restaurant. She doesn't care that Preston is there, either, because with Max beside her, it all just seems fun.

Then, hardly five seconds later, Preston walks past them going the opposite direction. He walks purposefully, as if on a mission, and again, he doesn't notice them.

"What is he doing?" Max says.

"I have no idea," Milla says.

Then Max says, "Look," and points out the restaurant's big glass window. Preston is *on the other side* of the window. *Preston is* outside *the restaurant!*

"Where is he *going?*" Max says.

"I have no idea!" Milla says, and she starts giggling again. What an odd night. And anyway, who goes out to eat with his family and then randomly leaves the table to wander to some other store?

He disappears from sight. The waitress drops off more breadsticks at Max and Milla's table, and Max and Milla both take one. As they eat them, they keep their eyes on the window.

"There he is!" Milla says several minutes later. He's clutching a shiny white bag, which he didn't have before. Whatever he's got in there is bumpy-lumpy.

"Is that a bag of *rocks*?" Milla asks.

"This is just weird," Max says.

"He's got to come back in the restaurant, though," Milla says. "Right?"

"Normally, I'd say yes," Max says. "But tonight ..."

A slight breeze lifts the fine hairs that have escaped Milla's ponytail. It's the breeze of a door whooshing open, and Milla glances at Max. They both turn to look, and yes, it's Preston! He hurries past their table for what's now the third time, and he still doesn't notice them. He goes so fast that Milla has no chance to solve the mystery of his bumpy-lumpy bag. Just that it's ... bumpy-lumpy.

"Miss?" Preston calls out to a random waitress. "Um, miss? Ma'am?"

Omigosh. Weirder and weirder, and Milla has to fight to keep her giggles inside her. Then something touches her under the table. Something warm. Something that fumbles around like a small woodland creature foraging for food—only not a scary woodland creature or one with claws. Not a woodland creature at all, but a hand.

Max's hand! Max's hand finds Milla's, and he laces his fingers through hers and he squeezes. As for Milla? Omigosh, she would *totally* giggle if she could. But again she doesn't, only this time it's not to keep Preston from spotting them. This time it's because her throat has closed so suddenly ... *zwoop!* ... that it's formed an (almost) airtight seal.

It's all right, though. Everything's more than all right, and the reason she's incapable of giggling isn't because she's stressed. It's the opposite.

"Ma'am?" Preston says more urgently. Milla gives Max

a delighted look. *What is this nutball doing?* they ask each other without words.

"Ma'am!" Preston calls, jogging up behind a waitress. The waitress jumps. Milla jumps, too, and this time she squeezes Max's hand.

"Oh!" the waitress says. "Can I, ah . . . ?" She keeps walking, her tray held aloft. "Can I help you, little guy?"

"Little guy," Max whispers.

"Hee hee," Milla whispers back. *Little guy!* Preston must hate that. For a millisecond, Milla wishes Katie-Rose was with them to enjoy this strange, strange play unfolding before them. Then, loving the warmth of the hand in hers, she realizes she most definitely does not.

"Yeah, listen," Preston says to the waitress, keeping pace with her as she strides across the carpeted floor. "I was wondering if you could *mumble-bumble-bumble . . .*"

They exit the room together, Preston and the waitress. Milla glances at her and Max's moms. They're chatting comfortably, each with a glass of red wine in her hand. They seem to be giving Max and Milla their own space, for real this time.

"Could you hear what he said?" Milla asks Max.

Max shakes his head. "Nip. You?"

Nip? Milla frowns. *Ohhhhh.* That silly Max.

"Nip, me neither," she says. "Oh well."

"Breadstick?" Max says, offering her the basket with his free hand.

"Why, thank you," Milla replies.

Thursday, November 11, 9:33 PM
To: Yasaman Tercan
From: Camilla Swanson
Subject: You were right!!!!

Yaz!!! I know you're prolly in bed already, and I should be too, but I had THE BEST NIGHT EVER!!!! And I just wanted to tell you that you were right: It *does* pay off to be brave. Omigosh, you were soooooooooo right.

Anyway, dinner was awesome . . . and I don't mean the food! Hee hee. The best part? We had FUN. Max and I. Despite all the weird stuff that happened at the restaurant—and plenty of weird stuff happened, believe me—we just . . . had fun. And laughed. And once? Well . . . I think his hand touched mine!!!!

Okay, fine. It did. His hand DID touch mine. You forced it out of me!!!! HE HELD MY HAND, YAZ! Under the table! And it wasn't gross or yucky at all. It was . . . romantic!

That's all. I just wanted you to know, because, ya know, you helped me.

Thank you. And I love you.

xxx,
Milla

Friday, November 18

Nineteen

Katie-Rose

*O*kay, just what is going on here, people?
That is what Katie-Rose wants to know. She surely
does, yip yip yip. And "yip" means "yup," and "yup" means
"yep," just for the record. "Yip" is Katie-Rose's fun expression for the day. She made it up yesterday on accident, but
this morning she invented an exciting variation called
yiperee, Bob!, which she plans to use with a certain FFF
who has hair the color of sunflower petals and whose
name is Camilla.

In Katie-Rose's mind, the scene will play out like this:

FADE IN:

INTERIOR RIVENDELL ELEMENTARY–HALLWAY OUT-
SIDE MR. EMERSON'S ROOM–MORNING

KATIE-ROSE

Hey! Milla! Hold up there, ol' buddy, ol' pal!

Camilla, an attractive young lady with hair suggestive of
sunflower petals (only pulled back in a neat ponytail and
not all wild like sunflower petals), turns around. She is
humming. She looks surprised at first and then happy to
see her friend, who is also an attractive young lady, but
with hair the color of a raven's wings.

She stops humming and beams.

CAMILLA

Hello there, Katie-Rose! You certainly look nice
in your jeans and your Paul Frank T-shirt with
the monkey on it. And may I say what a pleasure it is to see you on this fine day?

KATIE-ROSE

Yes, yes you may.

CAMILLA

(momentarily confused)

Oh. Well, great. It is a pleasure to see you! And if you want to know what kind of pleasure, I will tell you. A very pleasurable pleasure, that's what!

Katie-Rose bows.

KATIE-ROSE

Thank you. And likewise.

CAMILLA

And again: nice outfit. I should be more casual, like you. I know I was dressed up last night, when I saw you at that restaurant we both happened to be at—and wasn't that so random and weird? How we ran into each other at the Olive Garden last night?

Katie-Rose's eyebrows go up. She looks behind her, to make sure Camilla is talking to her. She looks back at Camilla.

KATIE-ROSE

That was *you*?

CAMILLA

Yes, you silly! You came up and talked to me. I happened to be eating a breadstick. And I was with Max, who also goes to our school. Now do you remember?

Katie-Rose gazes off into the recesses of her mind.

KATIE-ROSE

Oh! *Riiiight*. I knew there was something familiar about you!

Camilla shoves Katie-Rose teasingly.

CAMILLA

You knew it was me. Admit it! I'm not mad or
anything, Katie-Rose. Ha ha ha. Why would I be
mad just because we happened to show up at
the same restaurant? Ha ha ha!

Katie-Rose toes the ground with the tip of her sneaker.
She's sheepish in an adorable way.

KATIE-ROSE

Okay, fine, you got me. It *was* me at the Olive
Garden, and I *did* know it was you. Yiperee,
Bob!

CAMILLA

"Yiperee, Bob." Does that mean "yes"?

KATIE-ROSE

Yip.

Camilla cocks her head.

KATIE-ROSE

By which I mean yes. "Yip" means "yes," got it?

CAMILLA

Okeydoke.

KATIE-ROSE

And now that we've gotten that out of the way,

I have a question for *you*, missy.

Katie-Rose produces something from behind her back. It is a hedgehog! A tiny, fits-in-her-palm, stuffed hedgehog! It is extremely cute, and Katie-Rose has already named it and grown to love it, but that is not the problem. The problem is: Where did it come from?????

KATIE-ROSE (CONT'D)

Do you see this hedgehog?

Camilla takes a step backward.

CAMILLA

Why, yes. Yes, I do.

KATIE-ROSE

All right, good. Do you know where it came from?!

CAMILLA

Where it came from? Um . . . its mommy hedge-hog's tummy?

Katie-Rose rolls her eyes.

KATIE-ROSE

That's not what I mean, and stuffed hedgehogs don't give birth. Which you know. But did you know that this particular hedgehog of ador-ableness appeared mysteriously and magically AT MY TABLE LAST NIGHT?!!

Camilla gasps.
Katie-Rose nods.

KATIE-ROSE (CONT'D)

'Tis true! I speaketh not a lie.

Camilla gasps again. Perhaps she is perplexed by Katie-Rose's sudden switch into Old-Fashioned Language. Katie-Rose herself is confused by her sudden switch into Old-Fashioned Language. But she cannot—nay, will not!—let this stoppeth her! Eth!

KATIE-ROSE (CONT'D)

Verily, and it is so! The waitress came to our table to deliver our food, but spaghetti and meatballs was not the only thing she placed before me.

Katie-Rose emphasizes her words by thrusting out her hand with her wee and tiny hedgehog on it.

KATIE-ROSE (CONT'D)

She placed yon hedgehog beside my plate. *Right beside my water glass.*

CAMILLA

(uneasily)

Um, I'm not sure, but I think "yon" means "that thing over there."

KATIE-ROSE

(whipping her head around)

Over where?

CAMILLA

Over . . . oh, never mind.

Katie-Rose laughs. Her fingers close over her wee, tiny hedgehog of cuteness, and she thrusts it into the air.

KATIE-ROSE

I knew it! Is that your confession, then? "Oh, never mind"???

Camilla furrows her brow. She's wearing a silver headband to add glamour to her ponytail. It sparkles in the light.

Katie-Rose points at Camilla with her hedgehog-holding hand. Her index finger does the pointing, while her remaining fingers take care of the hedgehog holding.

(thunderously)

You! *You* gave me the hedgehog, yes? *You* gave the hedgehog to the waitress, and *you* said, "Hey, waitress, please give this hedgehog to yon girl over there!" Am I right, or am I left? *Hmmm-mmmm?*

In Katie-Rose's mind, the scene would end there. Or almost. In Katie-Rose's vision of how things should play out, Camilla would then swoon and say, "You're right! You're right! 'Twas I, indeed, who gave you yon hedgehog of adorableness! Yiperee, Bob!"

After that, the scene would fade to black, and . . . well, who knows what would happen? *Life* would happen, that's what. But life would happen in a clearheaded and predictable way, because the mystery of the hedgehog would be solved, yay and verily, yiperee, Bob.

The scene doesn't play out according to Katie-Rose's plan, however. When Katie-Rose asks Milla flat-out if Mona Bubbles came from her—because that's the adorable hedgehog's name, Mona Bubbles—Milla frowns and says, "No. It's cute, though."

"*She's* cute," Katie-Rose says in the hallway by the water fountain. "It's a she. I mean, *she's* a she!"

"Can I hold her?"

"No," Katie-Rose says, because she loves Mona Bubbles too much to let go of her quite yet. "And you did so give her to me. I know you did. You gave Mona Bubbles to the waitress, and you told the waitress to give her to me. Right?"

Milla gives Katie-Rose a funny look. If Katie-Rose were paying closer attention, she might note the way Milla's eyes widen and then un-widen, as well as the *ohhh, now I get it* smile that plays around Milla's lips.

If Katie-Rose were using her noggin, she'd have other clues to add to the mix, too. Not just from Milla's expression, but from Wednesday at school, when Katie-Rose used the SIHT fist on Preston, and everyone laughed, and Preston genuinely tried to say he was sorry. *Prickly*, Preston had called her when she refused to accept his apology.

And finally, if Katie-Rose had had the foresight to bring her beloved Sony Cybershot to the restaurant last night, and if she'd handed it to a super-sneaky invisible person and said, "Here, film everything important that happens over the course of the evening, will you?" then she wouldn't even need any of those extra clues.

She'd know the basics already, of course. She'd know, for example, that yes, the waitress at the Olive Garden honestly did bring Katie-Rose a small stuffed hedgehog along with her spaghetti. That yes, the hedgehog was— and is—ridiculously cute, and that yes, Katie-Rose loves that little hedgehog to the point of distraction.

But with the help of an invisible assistant and some well-shot video footage, she would also know that it wasn't Milla who snuck away during dinner to pay a hur- ried visit to Children's Toy World, conveniently located two stores down from the Olive Garden. She would know that it wasn't Milla who purchased a tiny hedgehog, and that it wasn't Milla who ran back to the Olive Garden, hunted down a bewildered-but-ultimately-agreeable waitress, and convinced said waitress to deliver the stuffed hedgehog to Katie-Rose.

She'd know that the person who wasn't Milla described Katie-Rose to the waitress like this: "So, um, she's a girl, and she's my age, and she's mainly weird, but kind of nice, only sometimes she gets super prickly, like a hedgehog. Get it? That's why I'm giving her a hedgehog. Get it? But you can't say who it's from! Um . . . *please*, that is. And she's short and skinny, and she's wearing a Krispy Kreme shirt, and her hair is sticking out from her head in two ponytail things, 'cause that's how she always wears it, and I think it's cute."

She'd know that the person who wasn't Milla then turned bright red and said, all in a rush, "And she's sitting right there, and . . . yeah. Thanks."

Katie-Rose, if she had access to all of that excellent footage, would turn bright red herself when she viewed it, and she'd turn bright red again remembering it.

But since Katie-Rose knows none of this, she's left in a state of extreme frustration when Milla shakes her head and says, "Nope. I think Mona Bubbles is very cute, but it wasn't me who gave her to you."

"Oh, come on," Katie-Rose says.

"You can believe me or not," Milla says. "But I swear

to God that I had nothing to do with it, and you know I wouldn't bring God into it if I didn't mean it."

"Well, was it Max?" Katie-Rose demands.

"Nope," Milla says.

"Was it your mom? Was it Max's mom?"

"Nope, nope."

"Are you sure it wasn't you?"

"Yep."

"Yes, it *was* you, or yes, it *wasn't*?"

"Yes, I'm sure that it wasn't me. Sheesh Louise! And it's time for me to go to class, so if you'll excuse me ..."

"But ... but ... *wait!*" Katie-Rose cries.

Milla turns around. Her lips twitch, and at last Katie-Rose is hit with a flash of understanding. Maybe Milla didn't have anything to do with last night's hedgehog delivery, but she sure knows *something*.

Now that she's really looking, Katie-Rose sees more in Milla's expression than that. She realizes that whatever Milla knows, she isn't planning on sharing with Katie-Rose, no matter how hard Katie-Rose begs. She realizes that Milla is quite pleased with herself about this, and she realizes that maybe—just maybe—she shouldn't have crashed Milla's date by "randomly" showing up at the Olive Garden after all.

"Yes, Katie-Rose?" Milla says. "Are you going to say something or not?"

"Um . . . not," Katie-Rose says.

Milla shakes her head and walks away.

Katie-Rose opens her palm and lifts Mona Bubbles up so that they're eye to eye. "You know who gave you to me, don't you?" she says.

Mona Bubbles is a cutie, but she's not much one for talking. She keeps her tiny mouth closed.

atie-Rose keeps getting mysterious deliveries of adorable little hedgehogs (stuffed, not real),
and not knowing who's giving them to her is driving
Katie-Rose crazy.

"Truly and literally crazy!" Katie-Rose says to Yaz after
the second hedgehog appears on her desk. And then, after
a third one materializes by the leg of her chair: "I am going
insane! Omigosh, I'm going to end up in an insane asy-
lum, and what if I'm only allowed to eat pudding? What
if I'm only allowed to eat vanilla pudding, or, worse, butterscotch?!" She pulls at her hair dramatically. "*Aaaaaah!*"

Yaz pats Katie-Rose's back and tells her that of course she'll help her figure out who the culprit is. Only guess what? During art class, Katie-Rose knocks over a metal can full of colored pencils—that's how flustered she is—and while she's busy picking them up, Yasaman sees Preston sneak over and place a fourth little hedgehog on Katie-Rose's drawing pad.

He winks at Yaz and holds his finger to his lips, and so Yaz keeps her mouth shut when Katie-Rose straightens up, spots the hedgehog, and screams. After all, the tiny hedgehogs are precious, and it's obvious that Katie-Rose loves getting them, despite her claims of impending insanity. After she screams, she clamps her hand over her mouth with one hand while sliding the hedgehog into her lap with the other. Their art teacher isn't in the room—she hardly ever is—and no one but Yaz saw what Preston did.

"Sorry, just a stabbing pain in my left shinbone," Katie-Rose tells the class. Several kids gaze at Katie-Rose, who flutters her fingers. "Carry on. Nothing here to see. Just . . . go about your business, people."

The hedgehog secret is a fun secret, though. The love

note secret was basically fun, too, especially once Yaz shared the details with Violet so that she no longer bore the burden of it by herself.

But a secret that isn't fun—a secret that makes Yaz wish she was *all done with secrets*—is how bad Violet made Yaz feel yesterday, when she ran off to save Hayley instead of staying with Yaz.

Yaz should have talked things out with Violet before her hurt feelings had a chance to grow inside her. But she didn't, and now those hurt feelings have gotten mixed up with the whole issue of Hayley—which isn't fair. Yasaman knows that. And yet now Yasaman doesn't know if she even likes Hayley anymore, and that particular thought is so heavy that Yaz feels helpless under its weight.

If there's one thing Yasaman has learned about herself over the past few months, however, it's that she is NOT helpless.

She can choose to be, or she can choose not to be, and while watching Katie-Rose stroke her bitsy hedgehogs, she resolves not to be. She wants to squeal and giggle and enjoy the day, too, without feeling weighed down by yuckiness.

When art ends, Yaz goes back to Ms. Perez's room, and soon she gets her chance to take action. It happens when Ms. Perez calls Yaz to her desk and says, "Yaz, sweetie, would you take this note to Mr. Emerson for me?"

Yaz says sure, even though Violet told her to say *no* from now on. Going to Mr. Emerson's room will give her an opportunity to have a whisper-chat with Violet, as long as she's not obvious about it.

"Here," she says to Mr. Emerson when she reaches his desk. "Um, for you."

Mr. Emerson's face lights up. "Ah, thank you, Yasa—"

"You're welcome," Yasaman says. She turns on her heel and marches to Violet's desk. Milla glances up as she passes. Yaz gives her a quick wave but stays focused on the task at hand.

"Violet," she says to Violet.

Violet is whispering back and forth with Hayley, but she stops when she sees Yasaman. "Yaz!" she says with a smile.

"Can I speak with you for a moment?" Yaz says. "Privately?" She makes eye contact with Hayley. "No offense, Hayley."

Violet gets up and goes with Yaz over to the reading nook. Mr. Emerson sees them do it, and he opens his mouth as if to tell Yaz to return to her class and Violet to go back to her seat. Then he changes his mind, it seems, because he shuts his mouth and shifts his gaze. Maybe he's slowly realizing that if he and Ms. Perez are going to use Yaz as their messenger, they can't get all that mad if Yaz pays a brief visit to her friend while doing their deliveries?

Yaz and Violet act like they're picking out books. They drop onto two beanbags and hold their pretend books (which are real, they're just not really reading them) in front of their faces.

"What's up?" Violet says. From behind the cover of her paperback, she wiggles her eyebrows at Mr. Emerson. "More notes?"

"Yes, but I don't want to talk about that. I don't have enough time. Okay?"

"Um . . . okay. What *do* you want to talk about? And why couldn't you say it in front of Hayley?"

Yaz hesitates.

"Oh," Violet says. "Is it *about* Hayley?"

Talk, Yaz tells herself. *Use your words.* And she does, even though it's scary. "Yesterday . . . on the playground . . . you kind of abandoned me, Violet. You just walked away."

Violet puts up no fight. "You're right. I am so sorry."

"I was talking to you. We were in the middle of a conversation. And you just . . . walked away! Is Hayley *that* great? Really? So great that you'd just, you know, pick her over me?"

"No!" Violet says. "I would *never* pick her over you, Yaz."

Yasaman's face feels hot. She drops her book to her lap. "Then why did you?"

"Yasaman?" Mr. Emerson says, feigning surprise. It's not very convincing. "Oh, excellent, you're still here. Would you swing by my desk? I have a—"

"Note for you to send back," Yaz and Violet say together. Violet laughs, and it breaks the tension. Yaz smiles a small smile.

"What did you girls say?" Mr. Emerson says.

"Nothing. Be right there," Yaz says. Her smile fades, and she waits for Violet to answer.

Violet sighs. "During recess, when I left you and went to Hayley . . ."

"Yes?"

"I felt like I needed to save her," Violet says in a hard-to-read tone.

"Um, okay. But you didn't need to save *me*?"

"You don't need saving," Violet says. "Do you?"

"Yaz, come on up here," Mr. Emerson says. "Time for you to get back to your own class."

"I felt jealous," Yaz says, speaking quickly. "I still *do* feel jealous. And—"

"You shouldn't," Violet says. "I went over there because I was worried Modessa was being mean to her. To Hayley." She drops her voice. "But I don't think she was, and then Hayley kind of acted mean to *me*—"

"She what?" Yaz says.

"*Yaz*," Mr. Emerson says, his tone suggesting that he's let her dillydally for long enough.

Yaz pushes herself up. "I'm coming! One sec!"

"But we worked it out," Violet says. "Me and Hayley. We talked, and . . . yeah."

Yaz doesn't know what that implies. *We talked, and . . .*
yeah? Yeah what?

"Oka-a-ay," she says, hating herself a little for what she was about to ask. "But do you pick me, or do you pick her? Like, if you could only pick one of us, who would it be?"

Violet's eyebrows pull together. "It would be you, Yaz. Duh." She pauses. "Do I have to pick?"

"Yaz. *Now,*" Mr. Emerson says, sparing Yasaman from answering.

She scurries to Mr. Emerson's desk and takes the note he offers. (Big surprise.) She tells him that yes, yes, she'll give it to Ms. Perez, and she leaves the room with her head down, not making eye contact with anyone.

In the hall, she exhales. She presses her back to the wall, and she stays there for two full minutes, or maybe even three. A whirlwind has passed through her, stirring up all sorts of emotions. She isn't at all sure how she feels about how things went with Violet just now.

When she opens her eyes, she opens the note, unfolding it carefully. She's done it once already, so why change her ways now? Anyway, maybe it'll be a good distraction.

Hola, John. I think our sweet little Yasaman might be reading our notes. Do you?

Yasaman's blood runs cold. *Oh, fudgsicle*, she thinks. But she keeps reading.

Hola, John. I think our sweet little Yasaman might be reading our notes. Do you? She's been looking at me in a strange way . . .
So she might be <u>on to us</u>, is what I'm saying. (!!!!)
What should we do?
xxx,
Maria

And then, from Mr. Emerson:

Yasaman? Yasaman Tercan? You think <u>Yasaman Tercan</u> is reading our personal, private notes?

Yasaman thought, after reading what Ms. Perez wrote, that she couldn't feel any worse. She was wrong.

Hmmm. I hope she's not, but she might be. And if she is . . .

Here it comes. Suspension. Jail, or possibly juvie, if they decide to have mercy on her.

What will her *ana* think, and her *baba*? And her elderly *büyükbaba* and *büyükanne*, and her gazillion of *halanin* and *amcanin*??? She will be a disgrace to the Tercan family name! Even after she gets out of jail, she will be put back in jail—in her bedroom! And . . . *oh my goodness.* Her *baba* will probably take away her computer. Not probably. Definitely. *Geez-o-criminy!*

She opens her scrunched-shut eyes and reads on:

. . . well, I can hardly blame her, can you?

What?

We are pretty fabulous, you and I. Fabulous, intriguing, mysterious. Compelling! Impossible to ignore! Undoubtedly the most epically spectacular couple in the twenty-first century, wouldn't you say?

Yasaman presses her lips together. *Really, Mr. Emerson? Really?* she thinks. He and Ms. Perez are adorable, but really?

And, let's face it. We <u>might</u> have set her up. Not on purpose, and Yaz should know better than to read anyone's private correspondence. Yasaman, of all people, <u>should</u> know this.

But she's a good kid. You know this, and so do I. I trust she does, too. Whaddaya say we cut her a break? To answer in the affirmative, simply don't reply to this note. We should stop anyway (delightful though it is).

See you at lunch.

—J

Yasaman has never experienced a last-minute reprieve before being shot to death by a firing squad. Yasaman has never faced a firing squad at all. But if she does, and if an official-looking woman runs to the Head Fire Squad Shooter at the last minute, murmurs into his ear, and then he commands the rest of the firing squad to put away their weapons ...

How she feels now is how she imagines she would feel if such a thing were to happen: Breathless. Light-headed. Hot and cold at the same time.

According to Mr. Emerson, she's a "good kid." As little as three days ago, she would have nodded vigorously and said, "Yes, yes I am! I *am* a good kid!"

Then came all the secrets.

Then came the firing squad.

Then came the official-looking woman who stopped the firing squad from firing.

Yasaman feels like she's been given a second chance at being the kind of person she wants to be.

She feels like she'd better use it.

❊ Twenty-one ❊

Camilla

At lunch, the four FFFs sit together, with no one else. Not Natalia ("I actually think Becca was looking for you," says Katie-Rose). Not Becca ("Natalia's over there. She's, ah, been looking for you," says Milla, softening the lie with a smile). And *not* Hayley.

"We're kind of in the middle of something," Violet tells her, fiddling with the plastic zipper on her ziplock sandwich bag. She doesn't meet Hayley's eyes. Neither does Yasaman, Milla notices. Milla herself *does* look at Hayley, but Hayley doesn't look back at her. Hayley is focused entirely on Violet, as if she's trying to unpeel her with her eyes.

"Um, okay," Hayley says. "No big."

She walks away and finds somewhere else to sit. Katie-Rose couldn't care less, based on her cheerful demeanor. But Violet and Yaz . . . Something is up with them. Yaz looks—well, surely Milla is wrong, but Yaz looks on the verge of tears. And Violet? Who turned Hayley away even though all along she's been the nicest to Hayley? Violet's mouth is a grim line, and her cheeks are flushed. Not just her cheeks. Her whole face.

What's going on? Milla wonders. *What just happened???*

"So, my friends, watch and be amazed," Katie-Rose says as she unpacks a tribe of teensy hedgehogs and sets them on the table.

One teensy-weensy hedgehog perches on the edge of the table. *Two* teensy-weensy hedgehogs perch on the edge of the table. *Three* teensy-weensy hedgehogs perch on the edge of the table.

"Whoa," Yaz says when Katie-Rose has unpacked six

teensy-weensy hedgehogs. Six hedgehogs and no sign yet of stopping.

"That's a lot of hedgehogs," Violet says.

"Yup," Katie-Rose says, and a childhood memory of watching *Sesame Street* floats into Milla's mind. She thinks of the Count, the purple Muppet dressed in black, with pointy fangs and a love for *arithmomania*, which for the Count just meant counting things.

He counted his teeth: "One teeth! Two teeth! Why do I have no more teeths?"

He counted potatoes: "One po-tay-toe, two po-tay-toes, three po-tay-toes, four! Five po-tay-toes, six po-tay-toes, seven po-tay-toes, more!"

Once, on a tiny little island, the Count counted coconuts. Another time, he counted cupcakes. Another time, he counted apples. "One! One apple! Two! Two apples! Three! Three apples! Yes! Yes, three apples!" And then his trademark laugh, which wasn't a *hah* but an *ah*, as Milla remembers it: "Three apples! *Ah ah ah!*" But then Cookie Monster stole one of the apples and gobbled it down, and the Count had to start his counting all over again.

Katie-Rose reaches nine hedgehogs, and Milla thinks, *Nine! Nine hedgehogs! Ah ah ah!*

That *has* to be all of them, or almost all of them. How many hedgehogs were in that lumpy bag of Preston's?!

"Why is everyone staring at me?" Katie-Rose says, though she knows perfectly well. She pulls out a tenth hedgehog and sets it on the table with the other nine. Milla wonders which is the first hedgehog Preston gave her, last night at the Olive Garden. She wonders if Katie-Rose even has an inkling that Preston is the hedgehog giver.

"What are their names?" Yaz asks.

"The hedgehogs?" Katie-Rose says. She beams. She goes down the line of hedgehogs, patting each one on the head and saying, "Mona Bubbles, Mona Bubbles, Mona Bubbles." Ten times she says, "Mona Bubbles."

"They're all named Mona Bubbles?" Violet says.

"Yiperee, Bob!" Again she pats her bitsies on their heads. "Isn't that right, Mona Bubbles? Mona Bubbles, Mona Bubbles, Mona—"

"We get it," Milla says. She isn't mad at Katie-Rose

anymore, but she isn't in the mood to let her go on and on, either.

"Why?" Violet says.

"Well, I will tell you," Katie-Rose says, in a special "important" voice she reserves for certain situations. A voice that implies, AND NOW I WILL BE SPEAKING OF IMPORTANT-NESS, AND I WILL DO SO FOR QUITE A WHILE, AND THERE WILL UNDOUBTEDLY BE SIDETRACKS. BUT THEY, TOO, ARE MADE OF IMPORTANT-NESS!

"The reason they are all named 'Mona Bubbles' is three-pronged," Katie-Rose begins.

"Like a fork?" Violet says.

"A fork," Yaz says. "Ha." She smiles at Violet, but it's an odd smile. A trying-too-hard smile?

There's something going on between Yaz and Violet, Milla realizes. She wonders what it is.

"Yes, like a fork," Katie-Rose says irritably. "Now, if you'll be so kind as to let me continue—"

"Right, sorry," Yaz says. She looks several tables over. "Only, why is …?" She cuts herself off.

"What?" Milla says. She cranes her neck and spots

Modessa and Quin at a table about five yards away. Hayley is with them. Okay, obviously Hayley went to them when Violet sent her away.

But *Elena* is sitting at a separate table all by herself. Well, there are two fourth graders at the far end of Elena's table, but they're not talking to Elena, and Elena's not talking to them.

"That's weird," Milla says.

"Does anyone want to hear about my three-pronged reason for naming my hedgehogs?" Katie-Rose says. "Anyone at all?"

Violet's eyes are hollow. She's gazing at Elena, too. Or possibly Hayley.

As for Yasaman, she's gazing at Violet. She looks miserable, and her chicken *shawarma* sits untouched.

"Maybe you could tell us later, Katie-Rose." she says. "I think we're all a little distracted. Right, Violet?"

Violet doesn't hear her. Either that or she decides not to respond.

"Violet?" Milla prods.

"Huh?" She comes back alive inside her eyes. "What?

Sorry. Um—yeah. Yeah, sure." She pauses. "What am I saying 'yes' to?"

"Nothing," Yaz says, casting down her eyes.

Violet knits her eyebrows.

Katie-Rose scowls.

Milla jumps in, saying, "Yaz was just suggesting that we hear about all the Mona Bubbles another time. She wanted to know if that was okay with you, Violet."

"Sure," Violet says. "Whatever Yaz wants."

Twenty-two

Violet

When lunch is over, the fifth graders storm the playground for afternoon break—and "storm" is the right word for it, given the chaotic flood of whoops and leaps and near-stumbles as kids hurry outside. "Storm" is the right word for Violet, too, although Violet's "storm" is a noun instead of a verb. Violet's storm is internal, and she stays inside the building as the others rush out.

Violet's storm is a dark gray tornado whirling in the place her lungs live. It whirls and sucks the breath out of her, and without breath, she can't speak. Without breath, she can't breathe, but okay, it's not that fierce of a tornado, or she'd be dead. *Thwonk*.

Losing the power of speech is bad enough, though.

Violet, without words, isn't *Violet*.

Violet, without words, is . . . anti-Violet. The opposite of Violet. A Violet-shaped husk, with a tornado inside instead of a girl.

"Violet?" someone says tentatively.

Violet is slow to respond. She knows that in reality, *she still is Violet*. Der. But she's Violet-in-a-whirling-daze, and it takes her a moment to pull the pieces of herself together.

"Yaz," she finally says. She feels spacey. She imagines two Violets, both of them paper-doll cutouts. One is the surface Violet. The other is the real Violet, if there is such a thing. The two Violets are stacked on top of each other, but their alignment is a hair's breadth off.

By now, Violet and Yasaman are alone in the commons. Violet, Yaz, and some crumpled lunch bags that didn't make it into the trash bag. Yasaman plays with the end of her *hijab*, a nervous habit that comes out when she's worried, and Violet has the ungenerous thought that Yaz has already yelled at Violet once today (not that she actually yelled). But is Violet going to have to hear about it all over again, how she's a bad friend for abandoning Yaz when Yaz needed her?

They stand there. They're within feet of each other, but the distance between them feels huge.

"It's Preston who gave Katie-Rose all those hedgehogs," Yasaman says.

Violet takes this in. Maybe she should care more, but right now, she doesn't. "Okay."

Yaz swallows. Violet can hear it.

Then Yaz sighs, and Violet can hear that, too. She also hears a rushing in her ears, and it's the gray tornado saying *wrong, wrong, wrong*. The rushing sound builds, and it hurts. Violet doesn't want to disappoint Yasaman, she doesn't want to let her friend down, but the rushing keeps getting louder until—*whoosh*.

It's gone.

Silence and clarity and the two Violets come together.

She doesn't want to let Yasaman down, but there is a right thing that needs to be done, and she, Violet, has to do it.

"Yaz—"

"Violet—"

They both break off. Violet smiles. It's a sad smile, but at least it's not fake.

"You first," she says.

"No, you," Yaz says. "Please."

Violet takes a breath, then lets it out in a fast flow of words, the tail end of a spent tornado. "I can't not be friends with Hayley. I can't ignore her. I can't tell her not to sit with us. You're my best friend, Yaz—you and Milla and Katie-Rose—but Hayley might end up being my friend, too."

"Okay, but Violet—"

"No. Wait. It's just, I can't treat her like Modessa treated me. Like Modessa *still* treats me. And I know, *I know*, Hayley's her own person. She's a big girl, and she can take care of herself. But can she? Or is that just something people like to say?"

"Well, what *I* was going to say—"

"Only I'm not sure it even matters," Violet goes on, "because if I turn my back on Hayley, then I'm no better than Modessa. And I'm sorry, Yaz, but I am. I'm better than Modessa. So are you. So are all of us."

"I know," Yaz says.

"And Hayley's new, and she's had, like, a hard life, and maybe she isn't perfect, but she isn't an Evil Chick, either. Only what if she turns into one, and it's our fault?"

"Well, it wouldn't exactly be *our* fault," Yaz says. "Like you said, Hayley's her own person . . . so wouldn't it be *her* fault if she chooses to be an Evil Chick?"

Violet narrows her eyes a little.

Yaz says, "But . . . that's not really what I meant to say. I mean . . . go on. Sorry."

"Take, for example, lunch today," Violet says. "We told Hayley to go away, and she did, and she ended up with Modessa and Quin. She ended up with them, and *Elena* got left out. And sure, Modessa made that happen—she kicked Elena out or whatever—but we helped. We were part of it."

"Kind of, I guess," Yaz says.

"And that made me . . . it made me feel sick. I'm not saying she has to be a flower friend. But she's still a person, Yaz, and I think she needs friends. I think she needs *us*."

Yasaman closes the distance between Violet and herself. "*I know*," she says. "I don't agree with everything you said, not totally. But I do think that we should be kind to her, and that's what I wanted to say, too."

"You . . . you did?"

Yaz puts her hands on Violet's shoulders. She steers her to a chair and makes her sit. She pulls over a second chair and sits beside her.

"I was wrong," Yaz says. "I said you had to pick me or Hayley, but that's not who you are. That's *never* been who you are."

"Huh?"

"You're not someone who sits back and stays quiet when bad things happen," Yaz says. Her voice is thick with shame. "And I made you. And I'm sorry."

"Oh." Three minutes ago, Violet's words were stuck inside of her. Then they came whooshing out. Now all she's got left are the single-syllable ones, like *huh* and *oh*.

"And I'm not the sort of person who looks away when someone needs help," Yaz says. "Or . . . I don't *want* to be."

"You're not," Violet says. "You're really and truly not."

Tears well up in Yasaman's eyes.

"Don't cry!" Violet exclaims. Tears fill *her* eyes, and she laughs and swipes them away with the back of her hand. "Don't you dare cry, Yasaman! You are the nicest girl I know, I swear to God. Or Allah. Or Bob, as Katie-Rose would say."

Violet makes a silly face, and Yaz manages a choky laugh, too.

"Okay. Stopping." Yaz presses the heels of her palms into her eyes. She drops her hands and blinks several times in a row. "So, um, I think we should tell Hayley sorry for sending her away."

"For real?"

"For real."

Warmth fills Violet's chest. "All right. Yeah."

"We should keep trying to help Elena, too," Yasaman says. "Don't you think? Even if it's hopeless?"

Violet scrunches her nose. "Elena *might* be hopeless,

but I guess we never know." She pauses. "Oh, gosh. Does that mean we have to help Quin? And *Modessa*?"

"Um . . . I'm going to hold off on answering that one," Yaz says. "Anyway, first things first, right?" She stands and holds out her hand to Violet. "Come on, let's go find Hayley."

Twenty-three

Katie-Rose

fternoon break is an adventure, to put it mildly. It begins with Violet and Yaz pulling Hayley over to Milla and Katie-Rose and making an announcement. They've been talking to Hayley, and they've just discovered that Hayley—yes, Hayley—is a real live dancer who takes hip-hop lessons and everything. And guess what? She loves dance parties, and tomorrow she's going to teach all the flower friends some dance moves.

"It'll be at my house," Yaz says, "and I want everyone to come. Okay?"

"A dance party?" Katie-Rose says. "That's out of the blue."

"No, it's out of Hayley's head," Violet says. "At her old school, she and her friends had dance parties all the time. Just because we don't have dance parties—"

"—doesn't mean we shouldn't," Yaz finishes. She and Violet grin at each other. Then she gets stern and focuses back on Katie-Rose. "We're doing it. It'll be fun."

"Um . . . okay," Katie-Rose says. After all, a dance party *could* be fun, she supposes. Plus, she kind of feels like she needs to be on her best behavior. Milla was surprisingly chillaxed at lunch—about the whole Olive Garden thing last night. Katie-Rose kept expecting her to bring it up. But she didn't. So Katie-Rose thinks maybe she should . . . be agreeable? Say thank you?

Violet explains that the dance routine will incorporate hip-hop moves with mock-cheerleader silliness. Then she clears her throat and says that she, personally, thinks the song they do their dance to should be the awesomely ridiculous "Sexy and I Know It."

"What? No!" Yaz cries. She swats Violet. "When did you come up with *that* idea, Violet?"

"It's a good song!" Violet protests. "It's got a good beat for dancing!"

"It *is* very danceable," Hayley says.

"But, Violet," Yaz says. "My mother. Will. *Freak*. She will freak! I am already freaking!"

"Me, too!" Katie-Rose chimes in. "Ten-year-olds *are not sexy*. Gross!"

"Chill," Violet says. "We'll use the karaoke version and change the lyrics, and your mom will never know. Cool?"

"I think it sounds fun," Milla says. "And, Katie-Rose, you can add in *whoo*s. I know how much you love *whoo*-ing."

Katie-Rose mulls this over. She hums a bit of the song to get it started in her head, then launches into actual singing. "When I walk in the spot—*whoo!*—this is what I see. *Whoo!* Everybody stops, and they staring at me! *Whoo!*"

Hayley laughs a big, loud laugh, which makes Katie-Rose grin. Yaz hides her face and says, "Oh my *gosh*," which makes Katie-Rose grin even more.

"But we'll change the lyrics," Violet reiterates. To Katie-Rose, she says, "You can still *whoo*, don't worry."

Katie-Rose gives Violet a thumbs-up. Then, feeling magnanimous, she throws her arms around Violet and Yaz and says, "Group hug!"

Yaz pulls Milla in, too, and the four girls link their arms over each other's shoulders. Katie-Rose breathes in deeply, noticing how nice her friends smell all clustered around her: sweet, sweaty, peanut-buttery. Although the peanut-buttery might be her.

"Hayley, get over here," Milla calls. "We're having a group hug—that means you have to be part of it!"

"That's okay," Hayley says.

"*Hayley*," Yaz scolds. "You have to!"

Katie-Rose can't see Hayley's expression, but she hears the doubt in Hayley's voice when she says, "Are you sure?"

"We're sure," Violet says. She digs her fingers between Katie-Rose's ribs, making Katie-Rose yelp. "She wants to know if *you* think it's okay. And you do, right?"

"Do I?" Katie-Rose says.

"*I* think you do," Yasaman says.

"Me, too," Violet says.

Milla brings her face so close to Katie-Rose's that their

noses touch. "Of course you do. It's our job to do the right thing. *You* taught *me* that, Katie-Rose. Way back when you helped me escape Modessa's clutches."

And you helped me, Katie-Rose thinks. *All of you.*

"Um…you guys?" Hayley says from the sidelines. "I'm feeling a little dumb here. Just so you know. Maybe we could start working on the dance, and you guys could, you know, stop hugging?"

Oh, whatever, Katie-Rose thinks. She rises to her tip-toes and says, "Come on, H-babe. Just, you have to *swear* not to turn into an Evil Chick. Do you swear?!"

Hayley hesitates, and then she smiles and bounces over. It's obvious she wanted to all along.

Realizing that softens Katie-Rose's heart. Spotting Modessa off by the swing set, glowering and looking fit to be tied—or fit to wet her pants —fills Katie-Rose's softened heart with fizzy glee. *Ha ha to you, you Evil Chick!* she thinks. Beaming, she makes room for Hayley and cries, "Huzzah! Yiperee, Bob!"

"You're weird," Hayley tells Katie-Rose. To the others, she says, "Is she always this weird?"

Katie-Rose takes a big sniff of Hayley's hair. It smells . . . oddly familiar. "Your hair smells good. Like . . . something. Something good!"

"*Always!*" Violet, Yaz, and Milla chorus.

"Ha ha hardy har ha," Katie-Rose says, delighted. She really does recognize Hayley's hair-smell, but she doesn't know where from. She puts that thought away. "Only, Hayley, you haven't sworn, and you *have* to. Do you?"

"To not become evil?" Hayley asks.

"Not to become evil, yes," Katie-Rose says. She peeks again at Modessa. It gives her great joy. "But more specifically, not to turn into *an Evil Chick*. You know, like Modessa and Quin and Elena?"

Hayley snorts. "Is that what they call themselves? Please. I have *no* interest in hanging out with those girls."

Well . . . but you did, Katie-Rose thinks. *You did hang out with them, and not just once or twice, but on multiple occasions.*

Yasaman will get mad at her if she says that, though. So she says, "Work with me here, Hayley. I am glad you have no interest in hanging with them. That shows excellent taste on your part."

"Thank you?"

"You're welcome. But repeat after me: 'I will not ever become an Evil Chick, or bow down to an Evil Chick, or be associated in any way with the evilness of Rivendell's three Evil Chicks.' Can you do that?"

Hayley untangles herself from the hug. She straightens her spine, lifts her chin, and proclaims, "I will not ever become an Evil Chick, or bow down to an Evil Chick. Nor will I be associated in any way with the evilness of Rivendell's three Evil Chicks, unless it is to *bring them down*." She looks Katie-Rose in the eye. "Are you satisfied?"

Katie-Rose searches her soul and realizes that yes, she is. She really is.

"I am," she says.

"Good," Hayley says. She brings her hands together in a single, sharp clap. "Then let's get to work. We have a dance to learn."

The girls work hard to master Hayley's choreography, and Katie-Rose is flushed and happy when Mr. Emerson signals the end of afternoon break by ringing his giant cowbell. She's leaving the playground with the others when someone taps her on the shoulder. It's Preston. Her pulse quickens. She suddenly wonders just how sweaty she is.

"Hold up," Preston says.

She does, without really knowing why. Kids pass her on either side. Her flower friends, as well as Hayley, disappear into the building.

Preston tugs her off to the side, to the sandy area where the play structure is. "So, uh, has anything unusual happened today? To you?"

"The hedgehogs," she says under her breath. She *knew* it, but she wasn't *sure* she knew it, but now she is! "The hedgehogs!" she says, this time with gusto. "You did it! You gave me all those hedgehogs!"

"I neither affirm nor deny that allegation," Preston says, but a smile tugs at his mouth. "Do you like them?"

She adores them, but she's not telling *him* that. "You asked if something unusual happened, and the only unusual thing was the hedgehogs, so you just *did* affirm that alli-whatever. So, ha. What I want to know is why?"

"Why what?"

She wants to rip her hair out. Or his. Preston has

surprisingly nice hair, for a boy. It smells surprisingly nice, too. She got a whiff of it one day when she was behind him at the water fountain, and its scent has lingered in her brain cells.

"Why hedgehogs? Why me?"

Preston wrinkles his forehead. "I don't understand the question."

"Preston! *Aaaargh!* You do, too!"

Preston smirks. "Sheesh, you're prickly. You know what else is prickly?"

Katie-Rose gets a bad feeling.

"Hedgehogs," he says.

Katie-Rose blinks. "You're such a jerk, Preston," she says. "Did you know that?"

"Huh?" His smirk falls away. "But . . . you smiled when you got them. Every time. You smiled every single time you got one."

"Because I didn't know you were giving them to me to be mean," she says. She feels like an idiot. "But now I do, and guess what? I'll un-smile when I throw them away, every single one of them."

She heads for the building.

Preston grabs her wrist. He holds on even when she struggles against him. "Katie-Rose . . . ," he says.

"Let *go*!" she snaps. "You're *hurting* me!"

He releases her. She stumbles.

"Preston! Katie-Rose!" Mr. Emerson calls. "Come on, kids!"

"We're coming!" Katie-Rose calls back. "One of the pre-schoolers left a tricycle out!"

"Well, put it away and get to class," Mr. Emerson says. "And hurry!"

There is no forgotten tricycle. There's just Katie-Rose and Preston. Soon even Mr. Emerson is gone; Katie-Rose hears the *clunk* of the heavy door as it closes behind him.

"You're going to throw them away?" Preston says. He rakes his hand through his hair.

His not-so-bad-for-a-boy hair. His very clean-smelling hair, which she has smelled before. Like, when she was behind him at the water fountain one time, and once during art class.

"Hey," Katie-Rose says, figuring out something that

was bothering her earlier. Hayley's hair smelled familiar because *her* shampoo smelled almost, but not exactly, like Preston's. "What kind of shampoo do you use?"

"What?!" Preston says. He looks so bewildered, and so silly, that Katie-Rose's anger leaves her. Her *prickliness*, as Preston might call it.

She fights to suppress a smile. Preston sees and his features smooth out.

"My *shampoo?*" he says. He preens in a way that only he can get away with, sticking his hip out and putting his hand behind his head. "Don't you wish you knew?"

"Yes, which is why I'm asking." Katie-Rose makes a fist and punches her palm. "Tell me, bucko."

"I will, but only if you come a little closer," Preston says. He offers his cheek. "Plant one right here, sweetheart."

"A punch? You want me to punch you?"

"A kiss, dorkwad. You know you want to."

"*Ewwww!*" Katie-Rose says, and yet her feet—what are they doing, those unreliable feet of hers? They're moving of their own accord! They're stepping closer to Preston *and bringing her with them*!

Preston lifts his chin, taps his cheek with his finger-tips, and says, "One smooch. One quick smooch, and I'll tell you anything you want to know."

"You are so gross," Katie-Rose says, her heart thumping.

He waggles his eyebrows. "Am I?"

She gulps.

He taps his cheek again. It is just his cheek, after all. Kissing someone's cheek is like . . . is like . . . kissing an apple or a baby. Or a tree.

"Okay, fine," Katie-Rose says. "But just so you know, I am pretending you are a tree. Got it?"

Preston tilts his cheek to make it more accessible. He closes his eyes.

"Oh, crap in a can," Katie-Rose mutters. "You better not tell anyone." She purses her lips, darts in for the kill, and—

"*Preston!!!*" She hyperventilates. She sees stars. She swoons and almost faints, and *not* in a good way, and the reason why is because Preston is a dirty, sneaky rat! Because at the very last microsecond, when Katie-Rose's lips were *this close* to Preston's slightly chubby cheek, he turned SO THAT HER MOUTH MET HIS!!!!

"Geez-o-criminy, you freakazoid!" she bellows. "What'd you do *that* for?!"

Preston is beaming. He's bright red, but he's beaming. "My first kiss," he says. He clasps his hands over his heart. "I will treasure this moment forever."

"Well, *I* won't!" Katie-Rose cries. And yet . . . she might. She just had *her* very first kiss, too. Geez-o-criminy!

"Until we meet again," Preston says, saluting her. He walks away, a spring in his step.

"Hey! Wait!" she calls.

He looks back over his shoulder. "Yes?"

Katie-Rose opens her mouth—*the very mouth that touched his*—then shuts it.

I kissed a boy, she thinks. The words play over and over in her mind. *I kissed a boy. I kissed a boy. I. Kissed. A. Boy.*

"Ohhhhh," Preston says. He gives her the smarmy snap-and-point move he's so annoyingly good at. "My shampoo, because you *loooove* the delicate aroma of my golden locks."

Katie-Rose wakes from her trance. "Your golden locks?! The delicate aroma?!!"

"My mom buys it somewhere," Preston says. "It's organic, so you could drink it if you wanted to and not die."

"Great, Preston. That's so totally fascinating."

"I know, right?"

"And *so* totally helpful, since you haven't even told me what it's called."

"Lusty Lavender," he says, savoring the words.

He grins. She scowls.

Geez-o-geez-o-criminy.

Saturday, November 19

Ultraviolet

hey, peeps!

 Ultraviolet

Since this is the place on our website just for sharing

news, I wanted to say that I had soooooooooo much

fun at Yaz's today. Dance party!

Wh-hoo!

 Ultraviolet

Katie-Rose, you were rocking it out, girl. Nice whoo-ing!

+pretends to be Katie-Rose: whoo! whoo!+ +shakes booty

like Katie-Rose+ whoo! 😊

 Ultraviolet

and Yaz, omigosh. As far as dancing goes, u are a natural!

U brought the house down, girl!

Ultraviolet

Milla? u were, of course, adorable . . . but u always are.

every so often u seemed a little distracted, but that's cool.

were u thinking about Max? hmmmm?

Ultraviolet

If so, I can hardly blame u, given that a) Max is pretty

awesome and b) Katie-Rose wasn't doing much to make u
NOT think about Max, was she?

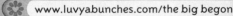 Ultraviolet

I mean, Katie-Rose, u seemed vair vair boy-crazy
yesterday!!!! what was up with that? I know u aren't mad
at Preston anymore, but is there something else going on
that we shld know?????

Ultraviolet

and why so much talk of kissing? Sheesh Louise! Or,
as u wld say, geez-o-criminy! Weren't u the one who
once said that WE ARE TOO YOUNG FOR KISSING? And
now you of all ppl are obsessed with Milla and Max
having some—what did u call it?—some "smoochie
smoochie" action?

Ultraviolet

yr prolly right that ONE DAY, Milla will be the 1st FFF to get
kissed. Whatevs. But we're talking one day far far in the
future, not right away!

Ultraviolet

but no, you had to go on and on about Milla and Max

and *kissing*. I mean, yr just plain weird, girlfriend—and
weirder yesterday than normal, which is saying a lot!

 Ultraviolet

but we love u, of course. +gives Katie-Rose a hug!+

 Ultraviolet

anyway, I had a blast, and I *know* Hayley did, too, cuz she
IM'd me and told me. so, thanks. thanks for including her
and being so nice to her and letting her, u know, kinda be
the dance party boss even tho she's new to our group, and
. . . yeah.

 Ultraviolet

I feel kinda dumb for saying this, because der! Of course
you were nice! but there's a difference b/w being "nice"
and being "kind," u know?

 Ultraviolet

one is just on the surface (nice), and the other is . . .
deeper. More for real. (That wld be kind.) And y'all were
kind. And it meant a lot to me, and I know it meant a lot to
Hayley, and now I will shut up about all that cuz I'm feeling
waaaaay too corny.

Ultraviolet

except I did also want to say a special thanks to Yaz for making a Hayley smilie for us. That is Hayley, right? Cuz of the red hair? And btw, isn't it funny, given her red hair, that her name is Hayley GREEN?

 Ultraviolet

Hmmm. Maybe it isn't funny. But . . . grass is green! And flowers live in grass! And that has nothing to do with anything, except, well, that maybe even tho she isn't a flower friend, she IS a friend? Like how flowers can be put in a bouquet—and that's US—but they grow in the grass, and grass is all around them, and the grass can be, like, Hayley and Natalia and Becca and Max and Preston and just . . . anyone?

 Ultraviolet

Am I trying too hard?

 Ultraviolet

I am, aren't I?

 Ultraviolet

Geez-o-criminy!

Ultraviolet

Last thing, I swear. I wanted to share my "Where I'm From" poem, cuz it's pretty much about you guys, and so it's dedicated to y'all, even tho I have to turn it in to Mr. E.

 Ultraviolet

Here it is.

 Ultraviolet

I hope it's not stupid. It probably is. But I mean every word of it.

<u>Where I'm From</u>

I am from words that come alive.

From a new school, and the smell of hospitals,

and three blooming flowers that sprouted in my path.

I am from the city of peaches,

but also the city of angels, or close enough.

I am from colliding together and bouncing apart.

From red hair dancing and bubble gum blowing.

I am from hedgehog love and sneaky missions,

from prickly hedgehog girls and one-day kisses,

but NOT anytime soon.

I am from the hallway of misunderstanding.

From bologna and water fountains and crumpled paper

bags.

I am from the art of crying silently.

From "sit here" and "come with us."

I am from Rivendell and its wide happy smile.

I am from Yasaman and Camilla and Katie-Rose.

I am from a garden with grass growing all around.

xoxo times infinity,

Violet

Acknowledgments

Thanks to Susan for being Susan and helping me write this book during a hard time. Thanks to Erica for being such a cheerful, tireless cheerleader. Thanks to Maria for making it look beautiful! Thanks to Zoey for liking me and getting feisty when my honor is challenged, and thanks to Bob, always, for ensuring that my honor—so connected to self-worth—stays intact. And, Al? I love your "Where I'm From" poem. Thank you for letting me model Violet's poem on yours! ♥

About the Author

Lauren Myracle *really* likes tweens and pre-tweens; she'd rather sit at the kids' table than at the boring grown-up table any day. She's written squillions of books, including the bestselling Internet Girls series and the Winnie Years series, and she is SO SUPER EXCITED about the Flower Power series. Why? Because at last she's written books that blend the thrills of social media with the goofy, wonderful madness of fifth grade.

Visit her on the Web at laurenmyracle.com, and come hang with Milla, Violet, Yasaman, and Katie-Rose at flowerpowerbooks.com.